LINCOLN CHRISTIAN COLI
W9-BUM-700

The Silas Diary

The
Silas
DIARY

GENE EDWARDS

Tyndale House Publishers, Inc.
Wheaton, Illinois

Visit Tyndale's exciting Web site at www.tyndale.com

Copyright © 1998 by Gene Edwards. All rights reserved.

The book of Galatians and the Scripture quotations in the text (from the books of Acts and 2 Corinthians) are taken from the *Holy Bible*, New Living Translation, copyright © 1996. Used by permission of Tyndale House Publishers, Inc., Wheaton, Illinois 60189. All rights reserved.

Library of Congress Cataloging-In-Publication Data

Edwards, Gene, date
    The Silas diary / Gene Edwards.
      p. cm.
    ISBN 0-8423-5912-5
    1. Silas (Biblical figure)—Fiction. 2. Barnabas, Apostle, Saint—Fiction.
3. Paul, the Apostle, Saint—Fiction. 4. Bible. N.T.—History of Biblical
events—Fiction. I. Title.
    PS3555.D924S55 1998
    813'.54—dc21   97-32269

Printed in the United States of America

03 02 01 00 99 98
7   6   5   4   3   2

TO
WENDELL C. HAWLEY
A friend, a gentleman,
and a man of honor

Gratis

113998

BOOKS BY **GENE EDWARDS**

First-Century Diaries
The Silas Diary
The Titus Diary (Fall 1998)
The Timothy Diary (2000)

An Introduction to the Deeper Christian Life
The Highest Life
The Secret to the Christian Life
The Inward Journey

The Chronicles of the Door
The Beginning
The Escape
The Birth
The Triumph
The Return

Healing for the Inner Man
Crucified by Christians
A Tale of Three Kings
The Prisoner in the Third Cell

In a Class by Itself
The Divine Romance

Radical Books
Revolution
Overlooked Christianity
Rethinking Elders
Beyond Radical
Climb the Highest Mountain

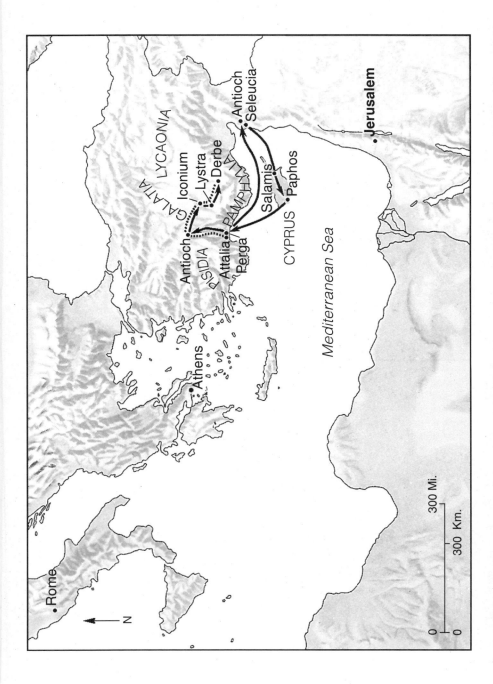

PROLOGUE

I have just received word that Barnabas is dead.

Paul rendered his life to the sword many years ago.

Timothy is in hiding and at the point of death—not expected to live.

At this moment a great deal of controversy swirls around Paul and Barnabas's journey to Galatia and the letter Paul wrote to the churches there. The controversy has grown to become a storm of fire. What caused Paul to write this letter? Only a few of us ever knew the story behind the Galatian letter. Of those who knew, only Timothy, Titus, and I are left. The whereabouts of Titus are unknown. He is feared to be dead. I have decided, therefore, to end the speculation—and perhaps the controversy—by relating the story to you.

I only regret that Timothy and Titus could not have joined me in this writing, for it is a nearly unbelievable drama. But as you read, bear this in mind: I, Silas, have lived in Galatia. I know the brothers and sisters there. I know what they went through. I saw the incredible miracle that Paul's letter wrought in their lives even at the moment of their greatest peril. I *know* the Galatian story!

If you remember nothing else, remember that I sat with Paul while he penned that letter. Further, Barnabas was one of my closest friends. I also traveled with Paul night and day for two years. I have heard both of these men tell the story of their journey to Galatia. Beyond that, I have heard John Mark tell his part of the story. He has recounted to me over and again the story of their shipwreck, and I have also heard it recounted many times from Paul and from Barnabas. As for Timothy, he has told me the part of the story that Paul and Barnabas did not see—that of the men from Jerusalem who visited Galatia. And to all of this I add my part and witness that what I tell you here is true.

Many copies of Paul's letter to the Galatians have been circulated throughout the empire. After you hear me out, I urge you to reread that letter. I daresay it will prove to be a totally new book to you. I pray that this story, and this new insight into that letter, will profoundly affect your life.

⌖

The story really begins at the time that some of the believers first went to Antioch. Luke has given us a brief description of the events in Antioch, including that momentous day when Barnabas and Saul set out on their journey that would take them to the province of Galatia:

> Among the prophets and teachers of the church at Antioch of Syria were Barnabas, Simeon (called "the black man"), Lucius (from Cyrene), Manaen (the childhood companion of King Herod Antipas), and Saul. One day as these men were worshiping the Lord and fasting, the Holy Spirit said, "Dedicate Barnabas and Saul for the special work I have for them." So after more fasting and prayer, the men laid their hands on them and sent them on their way.

When the two men began their journey, it started with a walk from Antioch down to the harbor located in the nearby seaport town of Seleucia. John Mark, the young nephew of Barnabas, traveled with Barnabas and Saul to carry their baggage—their food and clothes.

While the three men were standing on the pier waiting for their ship to set sail for the island of Cyprus, they were met by a beautiful surprise.

I shall begin there.

CHAPTER   1

What's that?!" John Mark asked, looking startled.

"Singing!" exclaimed Barnabas. "The brothers and sisters—they must have walked all night from Antioch just to come tell us good-bye. No doubt they've planned a royal send-off for us."

At that moment some five hundred believers from the assembly in Antioch appeared on the wharf, shouting and singing as they came.

"What a sight!" cried Saul as he ran toward them.

The three men melted into the throng. After several minutes of boisterous singing, they all edged their way along the pier until they came to the small freighter that was to carry them to Cyprus. Sailors and slaves moved aside to make room for the happy intruders.

"Oh no, not more food!" groaned John Mark as brothers and sisters began thrusting delicacies into his hands. "I've got so much food now that these sacks weigh more than I do."

"Make room for these passengers," shouted the captain. "But let no passengers board until I say. This Seleucia harbor is the choppiest in the empire. Even the hardiest sailors get seasick after a few minutes on one of these bucking ships." He paused, then added, "We will sail in a few moments."

Hearing these words, the believers from Antioch began singing a farewell song as slaves spread out along the pier, ready to push the ship away from the pier with long poles.

"Board!" cried the captain. "Find a place on the cargo deck. No passengers below. No fires. And remember, you provide your own food." Then he added, "It will be about six hours to Cyprus." He glanced at the sky, then muttered to himself, "If the weather holds."

Mark struggled manfully to pull his baggage aboard, even as some of the Antioch believers handed him still more food. The hoisted sails caught the early morning breeze. Barnabas and Saul rushed aboard even as the slaves began using their poles to push the ship free of the pier.

Shouts of encouragement rose from the throng of believers as the ship eased out into the churning waters of the man-made port. Barnabas, grabbing part of the rigging, swung up onto the ship's railing and began returning the brothers' exhortations. The Antioch Christians roared their approval. Saul smiled with delight, while Mark continued to wrestle with his baggage.

The freighter found the strength of the wind and began moving down the rock-hewn channel, tossing as if in a storm. Fading shouts turned to songs as the ship moved away from the port of Seleucia and out toward the restive sea.

"You'd better move toward the center of the ship until she reaches the open seas," said one of the sailors. "The tides in the channel make a ship buck like a horse. This port should never have been built, if you ask me."

"Six hours to Cyprus?" inquired Mark.

"With good winds," responded the sailor. "We're the very first ship out of Seleucia this year. The weather is *too good* for early March. Mark me, we'll pay for this good weather come April."

"Five denarii," interrupted the captain. "No food. No water. No going below. The deck alone is what you buy. Only if there is a storm will you be allowed below. Find yourselves a place somewhere among the cargo on the deck. Steal, and I'll throw you overboard!"

"Five days' wages for six hours of sailing," protested John Mark. "That's not fair."

"It's all right, Mark," explained Barnabas. "Some brothers from Antioch came down last week and struck the deal. It's pretty close to the usual fare and cheap when you consider we are the first ship out this year."

John Mark stared at his two overstuffed bags and then sat on one of them. Barnabas smiled. "I have an idea that when we get to Cyprus the saints there will be giving you even more food." Mark groaned, and Barnabas laughed good-naturedly. Then Mark's face suddenly lit up. Without saying a word he grabbed one of the bags and disappeared between the rows of cargo.

The ship broke out into the Mediterranean Sea, and Saul and Barnabas watched with intrigue as a small boat, full of young men, rowed furiously toward them. As the boat came alongside the ship, the young men began shouting wildly for John Mark. Mark peered out from the cargo, rushed to the railing, and shouted gleefully to his friends. One of the brothers in the small boat cried out to Mark, "We're jealous, John Mark. We wish you were back in Israel and we were on that ship." John Mark came back with a quick retort, but his words were lost in the wind. As Mark's friends turned back, they waved and shouted words of encouragement.

"Your first voyage?" asked a sailor who had been watching the small boat.

"Yes, sir," responded Mark. "We are followers of the Hebrew Messiah. We're on our way to Cyprus. Maybe we'll stay, but just as likely we'll sail from Cyprus to some other, uh, Gentile country. It all depends."

"Best not to sail beyond Cyprus. Not now. Not in April.

Spring has come too early; the seas are too peaceful. The gods will take revenge for this weather, be sure of that."

"Your captain said the same thing."

"Winter hasn't had her full say. She'll yet war with Spring."

"Now that we're in the open sea," Mark responded, "the ship's quiet, and there's no chance of seasickness. Would you happen to be hungry?"

"I was hoping you'd ask," the sailor responded. "I saw your generosity to some of the other sailors."

Barnabas and Saul had moved to the bow of the ship and were staring out at the calm sea. "That was quite a farewell they gave us," said Barnabas.

"Too nice for young Mark," laughed Saul. "But it's to be expected of those spirited Antioch believers."

Barnabas grew pensive. "It will not be so warm a welcome on Cyprus. For me, yes, but perhaps not for you." He glanced at his companion, then continued. "I expect there will be a good-sized group to greet us, but they will be a more restrained people. The holy ones who live on Cyprus are quite reserved. It wasn't like that at first—right after Pentecost. When the Cypriots who were in Jerusalem at Pentecost came back home to Cyprus, they were on fire. They spoke to just about every Hebrew on the island. But the glory of Pentecost has faded.

"Part of it is an island mentality. Those who live on a small island with a small population of their own people—well, they tend to be very conservative. The rest is our culture. We Hebrews are not as exuberant as the Gentiles in Antioch." Barnabas shrugged his shoulders. "I forget how different it is until I leave Antioch and move again among the Hebrews."

"I have a feeling you and I are going to miss the Antioch believers while we're gone," rejoined Saul.

"Saul, are you ready for a cool reception on Cyprus? Many of the believers are still not sure you have become a true follower of the Lord Jesus. They still think it's possible you're among us only to learn our ways, turn on us, and . . ."

"I know," came Saul's steady reply.

"I will testify on your behalf, of course, but . . ."

"As you have so many times before, starting with the very first time I visited Jerusalem."

"Still, some will not believe even my words. You will be confronted. Many still bear the scars they received during the persecution when you attacked the assembly in Jerusalem."

Saul stared silently across the waters for a moment, then shut his eyes. "I'm ready," he said quietly.

Musing about what might lie ahead, Saul returned to silence. Leaning back against a bag of grain, he closed his eyes. They had been up nearly all night with a small group of believers, who had accompanied them to Seleucia the day before. He smiled as he thought of their songs and their heartfelt prayers. As the sun warmed him, he drifted into a light sleep.

Several hours later, John Mark reappeared. "Are either of you hungry? I've got lots of . . ."

Barnabas laughed while Saul sat up and rubbed his eyes. "One sack is almost empty!" exclaimed Barnabas. "Did you eat it all?"

"No!" protested Mark. "I gave it to the sailors and the other passengers. They've got enough food to last them a week, and I've still got more than I can lift, not even counting the satchel with the scrolls and the one with our clothes.

"Look," Mark said, interrupting himself. "Way out there. Cyprus! Can you see it?"

"Oh, for the eyes of youth," Saul replied wistfully.

"Mother says I'm related to half the Hebrews on Cyprus."

"Yes, my sister and I *do* seem to have a lot of relatives there," agreed Barnabas.

The captain steered the ship toward the left to sail south of the island. Barnabas stood at the rail, drinking in the sight of his homeland. "Look over there, Saul. We're coming under the island's long eastern peninsula. You can see the little village of Eloea on the lee side. Few people live this far out, and most of them make their living by fishing in these shallow waters. Those hills are called the Olympus Mountains. In another hour we'll see Salamis, on a beautiful bay at the base of the peninsula. The harbor is protected by the peninsula, making it one of the safest harbors in the world. Also one of the busiest."

"You sound like a sailor," said Saul.

"No, only one who grew up in a family that sold copper. But the copper was always shipped out of the port of Salamis, and Cyprus is a land full of sailors."

Barnabas searched the distant coast for familiar landmarks. Eventually the harbor came into view. A great semicircular pier on the left and right, reaching out into the sea, seemed to extend its arms in welcome. "The Italians and Phoenicians come sailing down from the north to Cyprus. Rather than sailing all the way to Egypt, they deposit their wares here. Then they load up with goods left on Cyprus by the Egyptians sailing up from the south. The Egyptians do the same. Whether Egyptian or Roman, everyone sells and buys here. Much of a ship's goods are bought and sold right on the dock, then transferred to another ship. What is not sold immediately is left with brokers, mostly Jews and Greeks. They sell to the islanders and merchants of smaller means."

Despite the sun, a cold afternoon wind cut into Barnabas's face. He pulled his cloak tight and muttered, "Winter hasn't had her last say, has she? Bad weather is in store for someone out there."

As the cargo ship neared the Salamis docks, small boats rowed out to meet it. Ropes were tossed down. The men in the waiting boats grabbed the ropes and began rowing back toward the docks, the ship in tow.

Mark stared out at the wharf. "Look at that! I've never seen so much stuff," he whispered.

The entire wharf was covered with bales of cotton from Egypt, sacks of grain of all kinds, and crates of a very precious metal called tin, which came from the mysterious island of Britain. There were piles of rattan, stacks of teak and other exotic woods, along with mounds of carob, fruits, vegetables, nuts, and seeds. Bolts of linen from the Orient were stacked head high. But most of all, there were copper bars—cross-stacked higher than a man could reach. Cabinets and other fine furniture, to be sold to Italian merchants for the rich households in Rome, rested under protective canopies. And dotted all along the wharf were artisans, making and selling their wares.

"I didn't know Italy and Egypt could produce so much," said Saul.

"Actually, the Phoenicians have long trade routes. They circle the entire Mediterranean, stopping at every port in existence, buying and selling. Then they bring it here. What you see is really from all over our world."

❦

As the freighter pulled closer to its berth, Barnabas pointed to a crowd of Jews gathered on the wharf. "Look, there are the brothers and sisters." It was obvious that Barnabas could scarcely restrain himself.

A moment later the believers on shore began singing an ancient Jewish hymn of greeting. Barnabas's eyes filled with tears. "I can hear their Cypriot accent!"

Saul and Mark began to wave, but Saul could already see curious stares.

The ship's sails were struck, the ropes tossed to waiting slaves, who wrestled the ship to the pier. As soon as the gangplank was lowered, the three men disembarked and quickly found themselves encircled by well-wishers. Barnabas began reaching out to one and then another, calling names and receiving warm embraces.

"This is your cousin, John Mark. Mark, this is your great-uncle. This is my childhood friend. And who are you? Your face looks familiar, but I don't remember your name. How you've grown!"

Some in the crowd were calling out to Barnabas, "You must stay." "We need you here." "There is so much work to be done." "Cyprus has much need of you." "Please stay."

Saul stood back, silent and unapproached.

Much to Mark's relief, some young men picked up his luggage. "Scrolls, clothes, and food; be careful with the scrolls and clothing," he admonished. Mark watched with satisfaction as the young men struggled to lift the sacks of food.

After a few minutes, the band of Hebrew believers led their visitors away from the harbor and through a maze of narrow streets. They passed Salamis's famous racetrack, and finally their route led to a street barely more than a shoulder's width across. They stopped at an equally narrow door.

"We have rented this room for you three brothers. There is a sleeping mat for each of you. Sisters and brothers will come once or twice a day to bring food and meet whatever needs you have. When night arrives, some of the brothers will come to meet with you and share their hearts concerning Cyprus. John Mark, the sisters in the assembly wanted me to tell you they have prepared a great deal of extra food for you to take along as the three of you go out to visit the assemblies in other cities."

Mark managed a weak smile and a lame "Thank you," even as he watched the young men struggle to drag two particularly heavy bags across the floor. When their hosts had dispersed, Barnabas, Saul, and John Mark arranged their few belongings beside their sleeping mats.

As darkness drew near, men from the assembly in Salamis began to arrive. After a few minutes of formal greetings, the men began telling their visitors of the state of the faith in Salamis and across Cyprus. "We need you here very much," was the recurring theme. "None of the twelve apostles has ever come here. The assemblies are all small, and they are weak. We are so glad you are here. Please stay."

"Since those first days after Pentecost, when you all came back to Cyprus, have many other islanders become believers?" inquired Barnabas.

"At first there were many. Some of them are still with us. You'll be interested to know that every Jew on the island has heard the news of Jesus. The assemblies need you to gather some of these back. To speak to us. And to reach those who never believed."

Saul had kept his silence from the time he had arrived. His first words came directly to the point.

"How many Jews are on this island?"

"In all, perhaps a thousand."

"Followers of the Lord Jesus?"

The question turned out to be more difficult to answer than Saul and Barnabas had anticipated. But the answer was revealing.

"In the synagogue—many, perhaps most, are sympathetic to the news of the Messiah."

"In the *synagogue?*" asked Saul, clearly startled. "How many outside the synagogue?"

The men in the room exchanged uncertain glances. "Well, you see, the believers almost always meet in the synagogue on Saturday with all the others in the Jewish community."

"But," one hastened to add, "sometimes we gather in homes, too."

Saul repeated his question. "But how many believers are there apart from those who meet in the synagogue?"

The Cypriots looked at one another, not sure how to respond. "We don't know; we've never thought in those terms," was their consensus.

There was silence. Barnabas tried to assimilate this news, then struggled to find a way to respond. "We've been in Antioch a very long time," he explained. "We had just about forgotten that some of the Lord's people still enter the synagogue. In Antioch, the people who go to synagogue are *very* much opposed to the Way."

"Oh, that's not true here on Cyprus. The synagogue is our gathering place. There are a few *ecclesias* that meet in homes in small towns, but that's because there are no synagogues in the villages."

Saul ventured one last question, knowing the answer would dictate the entire course of their relationship to Cyprus. "How many Gentiles gather with you?"

"Gentiles?" It was evident that Saul's question was rather unfathomable.

"Don't any seekers from among the heathen nations ever come to your assemblies? Are there any *Gentile* believers?"

"Well, no, I don't think there are," responded one of the brothers.

"There is one Gentile, I'm told, in the ecclesia in Tamassus," inserted another. "At least I think that is what I heard."

Saul stumbled over his response. "All the believers on Cyprus—they are *all* Hebrews?"

Again the local brothers exchanged wondering glances. "Uh, yes. Why do you ask?"

Lest silence engulf the room, Barnabas changed the subject. "I understand the brothers and sisters here plan to gather early tomorrow morning. Perhaps we should all get some sleep. Will someone come to lead us to the home where we will meet?"

"Yes, but we will be meeting in the synagogue."

"The synagogue!" Saul nearly choked on the word.

"Yes, the manager of the synagogue is very willing, and he may even come to the meeting. Saul, he thinks he may have met you years ago in Jerusalem. He wanted to know if you were ever a student under Gamaliel."

Saul stifled a groan.

"Everyone is expecting you to speak to us, Barnabas. And Saul, as you know . . . well, there may be questions."

"It's very late," observed Barnabas again.

"Before we go, may we tell you of our plans for your travel?" asked one of the brothers.

"Of course," replied Barnabas.

"You will go from here to the town of Citium, on the southern coast. It's a two-day journey in good weather. The brothers and sisters from the ecclesias in the towns of Tamassus, Ledra, Kyrentia, and Lapithus will come to Citium to be with you. Everyone is excited. You will stay with the holy ones in Citium through the Sabbath and the Lord's Day. From Citium you will continue south and west to Curium. There is a strong body of believers in Curium. From there you will go on to the western end of the island, to the capital city of Paphos.

"One of the brothers in Paphos is seeking to arrange for Saul to have an audience with the proconsul, Sergius Paulus. It's our hope that by the time you reach Paphos, you will have decided to stay with us on Cyprus. We need your encouragement."

The meeting closed. A moment later Barnabas, Saul, and John Mark were alone.

"No Gentiles! Did you hear that?" Saul could hardly believe his own words. "Barnabas, they said there are *no* Gentiles in the assemblies! A thousand Jews on this island, and they've all heard of the Lord. The Jews all know God's good news, but these believers have no interest in speaking to the Gentiles about the Lord!"

"Unless they recognize that the Gentiles have also been

marked out for redemption . . . I'm afraid there's not much for us to do here," sighed Barnabas. "Encourage! We can encourage, but not for an entire lifetime! God did not call us to encourage. He called us to take the good news to the heathen nations."

"I'm glad to hear you say that," answered Saul. "I didn't want to have to remind you that when we knelt in that room in Antioch with Lucius, Manaen, and Simeon, the Holy Spirit sent us to the Gentiles. *Sent.* To Gentiles. To declare Jesus Christ to them and bring those who believe into the ecclesia. *What are we doing here?*"

Saul bit his next words. "We were sent to bring Gentiles not into a religious building but into the body of Christ!"

"I love this island," Barnabas responded. "My people are here. It is my home. I've dreamed of seeing a vibrant, living assembly on this island. But until the believers here understand that the good news is for the heathen, too, this is not where we belong. I'm afraid we would do great harm and bring much division if we sought to reach the Gentiles living on Cyprus. Confusion and damage would be everywhere."

"Good. Then let us go to the Gentiles. Let us find our way to places where neither Gentile nor Jew has ever heard the name of Jesus."

Barnabas sighed. "So be it. Tomorrow we will begin inquiring as to exactly where the gospel has reached and where it has gone no farther. *That* place, wherever it is, *that* is where we belong. Now, let's get some rest. The meeting begins at sunrise!"

"In a synagogue!" moaned Saul. "Synagogues are where I preach to unbelievers and where I get beaten, not where I preach to believers. Tell me, Barnabas, when was the last time you were in a synagogue?"

"Hmmm. About four years ago, just before I left Jerusalem for Antioch."

"What were you doing in a synagogue?"

"Asking permission to make copies of some of the Hebrew scrolls they keep locked up there. I am a Levite, you know. I have the right to ask."

"Did they let you?"

"Of course not! And you? When were you last in a synagogue?"

"In Tarsus."

"What were you doing in a synagogue in Tarsus?"

"I was there for the same reason you were. After all, I *am* a Pharisee!"

"Did they let you copy any of their scrolls?"

Before Saul could even think to answer, both men were convulsed in laughter. "I suggest I am not Levite enough, nor are you Pharisee enough, to satisfy our conservative Jewish brothers."

"How fortunate!" rejoined Saul.

C H A P T E R   2

Torches lit the dark, windowless synagogue, which was now
filled with believers quietly waiting for Barnabas to speak.
Barnabas, in turn, was thinking about Antioch and the rowdy
meeting the Gentiles were having just about this same time.

He stood to speak.

Everyone present was soon in awe as Barnabas told the
story of the church in Antioch. But when he recounted the story
of Saul's conversion, the room became deathly still. Only a few
dared even to glance at Saul.

Barnabas ended the Antioch story and began ministering
Jesus Christ to his listeners. Finally, Barnabas introduced Saul.
Since Saul recognized the problem his presence had created, he
gave a simple greeting, then offered his deepest regrets for all
the pain and sorrow he had caused to the believers in Jerusalem
more than a decade earlier.

Someone rose. "My father died as a result of the beating he
received in Jerusalem. He received those lashes in the synagogue where you tried him. I saw it. Then I, too, was beaten.
Thirty-nine lashes." The words were angry.

"Please," interrupted Barnabas.

"No, let him continue," responded Saul.

"I have nothing more to say, except that it will take more

than words out of your mouth to cause me to believe you are a follower of Jesus."

An awkward silence ensued until someone began a psalm. The meeting ended, and it seemed everyone wanted to get out as quickly as possible. A few did tarry to talk with Barnabas. One or two approached Saul, apologized for the outburst, but then began telling of their own suffering at his hands. They then asked if the story they had heard was true—that he had been struck down on the road *and* had seen the Lord.

At that point the man who had spoken so angrily walked up to Saul. Once more everyone still remaining in the room fell silent. "I am Carmi, of the tribe of Reuben."

"I am Saul, of the tribe of Benjamin."

Carmi turned his back to Saul, then dropped his cloak to his waist, exposing the deep scars on his back. "This is what you have done to me," he said bitterly. He then turned and began walking away.

"Carmi, wait." It was the commanding voice of Barnabas. Barnabas moved to Saul's side.

"No," Saul protested.

"Quiet," Barnabas commanded Saul. "Carmi, come." With those words, Barnabas stepped behind Saul and pulled at Saul's toga. Everyone gasped. Saul's back was a ribbon of scars.

"Damascus. The synagogue. Saul's stripes, as yours, came from the hands of Hebrew kinsmen. Saul's back is scarred for the same reason as yours, Carmi: for believing that Jesus is the Messiah."

Saul quickly pulled his garment back up over his shoulders. "It was nothing, and only once."

"Later he had to escape Damascus by way of its walls, in a large basket!" added Barnabas.

Several of the men who had not yet spoken to Saul came to him and embraced him. Together they hugged, and together they wept. Carmi slipped out without a word.

Early the next morning the three men, in the company of others, prepared to depart Salamis for Citium. Just as they reached the outskirts of the city, several sisters arrived, carrying food for the journey. A bemused Barnabas thanked them for their thoughtfulness, while Mark grimaced at the sack they held out to him.

Barnabas pointed toward Mark. "Yes, do give it to my young nephew. He is in charge of carrying our food, water, and clothing."

"A *third* sack of food," Mark muttered under his breath.

"The journey is all uphill. Your progress will be slow, but there is a way station between here and Citium," explained one of the men. "It is several hundred years old but adequate. As you travel, watch out for soldiers, as they frequent this area. Otherwise, your chances of a safe journey are rather good."

"What do you mean, *rather* good?" asked Mark as he struggled to sling the sacks onto his shoulders.

"Robbers are fairly rare on Cyprus. Besides, your journey takes you on one of the safer roads. It is the soldiers you want to avoid, especially those with chariots. They can order you to do anything."

"Even if you are a citizen of Rome?" pressed Mark as he glanced at Saul.

"Yes, Mark, even a citizen of Rome," assured Saul.

The brothers and sisters from Salamis walked up the sloping road for a few miles with their three brothers. Then, as steeper hills beckoned, they bade the three sojourners good-bye.

"Two of those sacks appear to be lighter than yesterday, young nephew. Is there any explanation for this wonder?" queried Barnabas.

Mark grinned. "Well, I didn't eat it! Let's just say I have many friends among the slaves who work the docks."

CHAPTER 3

Looking solemnly at the empty chariot abandoned on the side of the road, Barnabas observed, "The chariot of a Roman soldier. It's no use to him. It's broken, and he's gone for help. Pity the poor soul he first encounters. I hope he's taken a route different from ours. Mark, go ahead of us. There were two chariots here. If you see two charioteers coming this way in one chariot, come tell us quickly and we will hide."

Mark needed no encouragement but paused to say, "Uh, these bags . . ."

"Leave them. We will carry them for a while."

With that, Mark was off. By midafternoon he returned, assuring his two companions that the road was clear.

"We have made good time," said Barnabas. "We should be in Citium by late tomorrow afternoon."

"You said your family's former copper mines are near?" asked Saul.

"Near Tamassus, in the high mountains."

"Mark, do you see that bleached area on the side of that mountain? No trees, no vegetation. Look closely, and you will also see the mouth of a copper mine. Some of these mines are privately owned. The emperor controls almost all the rest. Do you see the soldiers? That means it's an imperial mine. The workers in the mines are all slaves, brought here from all over the world. Some are Phrygians and Gauls, but most of the slaves are soldiers of foreign armies who lost their battle with the Roman legions. They were shipped here to work the mines. When they arrived at the entrance of the mine, every slave was stripped naked, chained, and then led down into the mine. They live there in its dark caverns, never again to see the light of day. They work there, they eat there, they die there, and they are even buried there. Once a slave enters the mines, he never sees the outside world again."

Mark looked nervously above. He was about to say something when around a bend in the road appeared a chariot with two soldiers.

"Can he force us into the mines?" Mark asked.

"Not as long as there is a Roman citizen among us."

Taking comfort in Saul's words, Mark whispered, "Thank God."

"But there is much he can do," Saul said, speaking quietly.

Behind the chariot was a leashed horse. In front of the chariot walked two peasants and a slave, sullen but compliant, for one of the soldiers held a whip in his hand.

"Halt, there," ordered the soldier with the whip.

One soldier was young. The other, the one brandishing the whip, was older, of stout build, and on his hands, face, and body were scars of war.

"Those bags you carry. Bring them here," ordered the younger soldier as he drew his sword and motioned to a terrified Mark.

Mark approached the chariot and handed the heaviest sack to the older warrior, who recklessly rummaged through it. The soldier began pulling food out of the bag and dropping it on the floor of the chariot. "What's in the other bag?" he growled, speaking to Barnabas.

"Only clothes, those of a Jew," came Barnabas's wise reply.

The soldier swore an oath of contempt. "And yours?" he commanded Saul.

"The tools of my trade."

Curious, the young soldier stepped down from the chariot and approached Saul. He pawed at the contents of the crusty bag. "Can your tools repair broken leather?"

"It is part of my trade."

The older charioteer barked back at the peasants. "Be gone," he said as he brought his whip down hard on their backs. "I don't need you anymore."

The younger Roman soldier pointed back down the road the three men had just traveled. "Walk in front of the chariot," he commanded. "And be quick about it. We've got work to do, and it's getting late."

"This is wicked," said Mark, smoldering.

"Remember our Lord's saying, Mark. If a soldier asks you to go one mile . . ."

"But it's almost half a day's journey back to that broken-down chariot. That's *seven* miles, not two. Besides, I heard the Twelve say no one could actually live up to the Lord's teachings."

Silently, the three men retraced their every step. When they finally arrived back at the abandoned chariot, Saul set about mending the broken harness. An hour passed before his task was completed. Then he brought the horse to the harness and tested its length and strength. Without a word, the soldiers of Rome turned their two chariots toward Salamis.

"I haven't been that scared since Gethsemane," offered Mark. "We'll never make Citium by tomorrow afternoon. What are we going to do?"

"Barnabas, give me your luggage," said Saul. "Go on ahead of us. Try to reach the brothers in Citium by nightfall tomorrow. Mark and I will arrive sometime after you."

Barnabas nodded.

"But take some food and water with you," added Mark.

Barnabas smiled and then added, "Your thoughtfulness is to be admired." In a moment Barnabas had disappeared from view.

"Where will he sleep tonight?"

"Unless he finds an inn, he will sleep in much the same place we will."

"Where's that?"

"In an open field. Now, let's hurry. I feel the bite of an evening much colder than anything we have experienced since we left Antioch."

That night a Pharisee from Tarsus and a young man from Jerusalem spent a cold night in an open field on an island located on the eastern end of the Mediterranean Sea. They slept only fitfully in the cold. But it would not be the worst of their nights.

CHAPTER 4

By noon the next day a furious wind had blown in from the north. "A storm is coming," Saul said wryly.

"Do you think it will rain?" asked Mark.

"I had hoped it would hold off till tomorrow, but it will be today."

"Are we in danger?"

"Always, in weather that does not obey its own signs. Yes, Mark, we must move as quickly as possible. Find a way to lighten your load."

The two men shared their last light moment as Mark dumped the entire contents of one bag while thunder and lightning joined a howling wind. By nightfall the two men were seeing hints of snow and sleet.

"We can't walk much farther, Saul. I can hardly see the road."

"We walk, or we court death," was Saul's response.

"Do you think it's that bad?"

"Our only hope is the way station."

The men moved on in silence, pausing only to verify their way, sometimes finding it only by brief flashes of lightning. The temperature was falling.

"We are near, Mark."

"Do you see the way station?"

"No, but there are no trees—a sure sign we are near a way station. Let's pick up the pace."

The intermittent rain and snow were turning into unbearable sleet. "There it is!" exclaimed Mark.

Breathing hard, the two men passed through the unguarded gate. The lightning revealed a courtyard with three walls. The fourth wall was actually a series of windowless rooms. "It certainly *is* several hundred years old," muttered Saul.

In the middle of the courtyard were several men huddled around a large fire, all slumped and motionless. Saul walked over to the fire and began warming himself. Then he reached down into the satchel he had been carrying and withdrew two leather coats, each with a hood. "Here, put this on, John Mark." Saul put on his leather coat, moved as close to the fire as possible, sat down, and pulled the hood over his head. Then, like the others, he slumped forward and rested his head on his knees.

In the midst of the storm's howling sleet, Mark was confused. "The rooms," he said. "Why aren't we going into those rooms?"

One of the strangers stood, looked sullenly at Mark, stirred the fire with a stick, and then sat down again. Saul motioned Mark to his side. "There are no doors on those rooms, and there haven't been for at least a hundred years. The doors were ripped off a century ago and used for firewood. Also, the roofs leak. Further, no sane man would go in there. There may be thieves in there waiting to cut your throat. Or one might just follow you in there *after* you fall asleep. The floor is dirt, and the straw hasn't been changed for years. It is filthy beyond knowing. But worst of all, there are vermin and rats! The worst vermin are the lice. Now, sit down and try to stay warm until this freeze passes."

"But it stinks. The fire stinks."

"That's because what you see burning is dried dung. Now sit. I will take the first watch, you the second. Get some sleep."

Mark pulled his leather covering about him, lowered the hood over his head, muttered something, and fell silent. Soon the men were covered with snow and sleet. Late in the night the winds cut sharper, and the cold grew even more severe as the fire waned. Saul rose and left the courtyard to scavenge for wood. After a long absence, he returned to a fire not much more than embers.

"Sparingly—only a little wood at a time. It will still be a long night," said one of the men sitting nearby.

Hearing those words, Mark shot to his feet, said something about preferring to die swiftly at the hands of a cutthroat thief, and then stumbled over to one of the empty rooms. He stuck his head in one and then another, finally disappearing into one of them. Inside he pushed himself against one of the walls, lowered his head and hood, and waited for sleep to deliver him from his agony.

"Are you going to let him stay in there?" one of the men asked Saul.

"He must learn. But I'm afraid he has chosen a poor way to do so."

At the first light of day, Mark came running out of the room, screaming at the top of his voice. "They're all over me!" he cried, shaking his hair and hitting at his arms and legs. "But I can't see them. What are they?" he asked, walking right into the smoking embers.

"Lice," laughed an old man.

"What can I do to get rid of them?"

"You might try drowning yourself. Not too many lice can live at the bottom of the sea."

"Is there anything else I can do to get rid of these things?" Mark asked again amidst rancorous laughter.

"Shave your head," Saul answered honestly, but his voice betrayed his amusement.

The two men gathered up their few belongings, Mark giving to the other travelers all but the last of their food. "Next time we get a mule," grumbled Mark as the two men set out on a road now covered with sleet and water.

Late in the afternoon, cold beyond description, they finally arrived at Citium, where they were warmly greeted by the anxious brothers and sisters. They were quickly whisked off to the warmth of the house where they would be staying. Everyone, including Barnabas, who had arrived the night before, was amazed that Saul and Mark had braved this weather and lived.

C H A P T E R 5

On each of the next two nights the holy ones from Kyrentia, Lapithus, Ledra, Tamassus, and Citium gathered in the *trich-nium*, the living area of the house, to hear Barnabas and Saul. Time and again the two men heard the plaintive request that they remain on the island to help the churches.

On the morning of the third day, a breathless messenger arrived from Paphos. "I am from the proconsul's palace. A relative of yours, a Hebrew named Kala, sent me. He serves our most honorable proconsul, Sergius Paulus. The proconsul desires your immediate presence, for his term as proconsul of this island ends within a month. He wishes to hear from Saul of Tarsus before returning to Rome. Can Saul come immediately?"

Barnabas looked at Saul. "It takes precedence over other matters, I should think. But it will take us three days to get there. Is Sunday acceptable?" he asked the messenger.

"I will take your message to Kala. I believe Sunday is acceptable."

"We should leave immediately," observed Barnabas. "We'll go through Koukhia and arrive at Old Paphos by the Sabbath. New Paphos is nearby."

Saul was in a reverie all his own. "The proconsul of all

Cyprus. Very interesting. Perhaps this is the very thing that will aid us in our decision concerning Cyprus, to stay or to leave."

Mark was silent, his counsel his own. His only hope was that the sisters of Citium would not be too generous in preparing food for their journey.

Within an hour the three men had said their good-byes and stepped out into a misty night, following the road leading to the western tip of the island.

Friday afternoon, just before the Sabbath began at dusk, the three men arrived at the ancient city called Old Paphos. "There is only one family of believers in Old Paphos," they had been told at Citium. It was with this family that they found lodging.

"Word of your possible arrival has reached the local synagogue," their hosts told them. "You must stay away from the Old Paphos synagogue. The ruler of the synagogue, a man named Shedean, has opposed the Way from the beginning. It is only in Old Paphos that most of the Jewish community has not received its Messiah. It is Shedean's rage against believers that has stood in the way. Shedean has heard of Barnabas and of Saul's converting to the Messiah. He is *not* pleased. We counsel you not to go there."

Saul was unmoved. "Perhaps we will catch him on one of his good days," he suggested.

Early on the Sabbath morning, Saul ventured up to the door of the synagogue, sure he would be given an audience. After all, he was a Pharisee. To Saul's surprise, Shedean met him at the door. "Saul, is it true that you have accepted the teaching that Jesus is the Messiah?"

"Yes. And not only that, but I have seen him face-to-face on the road from Jerusalem to . . ."

"Seize him!" ordered Shedean. Three men waiting just inside the synagogue door suddenly appeared, grabbed Saul, and hauled him into the synagogue. Just as quickly, they pushed him to a whipping pillar about three feet high and bound him to it.

"We will beat this lie out of you, Saul of Tarsus," growled Shedean. "Let all see what should be done to those who follow a carpenter." Shedean took his place right in front of Saul, who was now held firmly across the whipping column. "As you are beaten by your Hebrew brothers, remember that you ordered hundreds in Jerusalem to be beaten in the synagogue of the holy city for the same crime for which you yourself are now guilty. Remember this with every lash, and then turn from your evil. Return to Moses."

Shedean nodded to one of the men standing behind Saul. With that, a whip with four straps appeared. The whip whistled in the air and found its mark, ripping at Saul's flesh. One by one, thirty-nine such lashes tore into Saul's already scarred back.

The beating ended, and Saul was thrown bodily out of the synagogue. He staggered back to the home where he was staying.

> Five
> different times
> the Jews
> gave me
> thirty-nine lashes.

It was because of that horrid day that the Hebrew believers on Cyprus gave up all doubts as to whether Saul was a follower of Christ. John Mark, who later spent many years on Cyprus, told me that there are many believers in Old Paphos today. Should you go there, those believers will take you to the very place where Saul was beaten for his faith. The pillar he was tied to is still there for all to see.

❦

"Bathe my back, and bind it well. Tomorrow morning there must be no blood seeping through my shirt. The proconsul of Cyprus must not see that I have been whipped."

"But, Saul!" protested Barnabas.

"I know," responded Saul. "When you remove the strips of cotton, the pain will be terrible and the healing will have to begin all over again. It matters not. There must not be so much as a drop of blood that shows through. Tomorrow, no evidence of this beating."

Kala, the man who served the proconsul, arrived early Sunday morning. "My master, Sergius Paulus, will see you at noon," he said.

"This audience, Kala—how did it come about? An unknown Jew before a Roman proconsul?"

"He is proconsul of the island, yes, and I am a slave; but we are friends."

"But why this audience?"

"Paulus is a botanist, a scientist of no small renown. He has a son living in Rome; his daughter lives here on Cyprus, in the palace. She is very interested in our Lord Jesus. As to Paulus, I am not sure. He is a thinker, but on the other hand, signs seem to play a significant part in his life. He is intrigued with the story of your miraculous conversion. You have only one thing to fear, Saul. That is, besides fainting from your wounds."

"Fear?"

"Yes, a rascal named Simon, who serves as Paulus's advisor."

"Simon! Yes, I know of him. He's an impostor—part liar, part Jew, part follower of Christ, and part magician, or so he claims. That man has a heathen's heart and a robber's mind."

"Yes, that is Simon," agreed Kala. "You describe him well. Sometimes he goes by the name Elymas, which means "sorcerer." And sometimes he even calls himself Bar-Jesus, or Son of Jesus. He will probably introduce himself as such."

Purple rage swept across Saul's face. "More to the truth, he's the son of . . ."

"Come, we must hurry. Getting into the palace is a task within itself. Remember, Simon is the consort of Paulus. He does not plan to lose his employment as a result of your being here to speak to the proconsul. He will oppose you to your face if . . ."

Saul was not listening. "Does Paulus know Claudius personally?"

"Uh, you mean Claudius the *emperor?*"

"Yes."

"Well, I think he does. Why?"

"Does he know him well enough to get me an audience with Claudius?"

"Are you mad?"

"No, I am a Roman citizen."

"Saul of Tarsus, there is room for a man to be a citizen of Rome and still be mad."

Saul smiled. "One day I shall see Rome. And perhaps the emperor—that is, if I find time to do so. Now let us go so that I might tell a Gentile, who also happens to be a Roman proconsul, the wonderful news about Jesus Christ."

"The rumors about you are not big enough, Saul."

Saul turned and faced Kala. "Never forget, I have seen Jesus Christ. Not as the carpenter of Nazareth. I saw the resurrected, ascended, enthroned Lord. What space can a mere proconsul from Rome—or this Simon—take in the presence of such glory? Now tell me, Kala, how did Sergius Paulus come to receive the honor of being made ruler of Cyprus?"

"Well," responded Kala, taking a deep breath, "when the Romans took Cyprus from the Greeks, there was discontent throughout the island. The emperor sent an army here, an army overseen by a man appointed as *governor*—a governor who reported directly to the emperor. When the people of Cyprus finally settled down and accepted their conquerors, the emperor turned Cyprus over to the Roman senate. No longer would there be a governor here, appointed by the emperor. The senate was in charge of Cyprus, and the senate chose someone called a proconsul to govern the island. The army was then removed from the island. This year the proconsul happens to be Sergius Paulus. I only hope next year's senatorial appointee is as kind a man as Sergius. May Cyprus like him, whoever he is. Cyprus wants no more of the emperor and his army. The people are happy to be ruled by the senate of Rome. Even a small garrison of guards and charioteers is more than enough for us."

"Our people in Israel have *never* had a senate-appointed proconsul," responded Barnabas. "Israel has always had governors and a large Roman army. We will probably never have a proconsul. Even now, hidden under the surface of the Roman-imposed peace, there is great discontent throughout Israel. Even now the emperor is sending in more soldiers."

"There is no such danger here," laughed Kala. "We learned our lesson."

At that moment the three men entered New Paphos. "See the port? It is new. It was built to serve Old Paphos, but a new city grew up around the port. The people of Old Paphos still resent the port and the new city. Look up there, on that high bluff at the very tip of the island. That's the proconsul's palace."

"Then let us be on time. We must not keep a proconsul waiting. We dare not start a Roman war," laughed Saul.

CHAPTER 6

Your Eminence, I present to you Saul of Tarsus, a citizen of Rome by birth, and a man of great learning, with a wide reputation for insight into the mysteries of the God of Israel." Kala bowed and retreated to the far end of the great audience room.

Saul flinched. A typical court introduction, true, but it did not suit him.

"Your name is Saul," responded Sergius Paulus. "That would make you a member of the tribe of Benjamin, named after Israel's first king, Saul son of Kish."

Saul blinked, caught wholly off guard. "You both astound me and honor me, Your Excellency. I had no idea you knew so much of the Hebrew story. There are many Jews who do not know these matters of which you speak."

"I am interested in several of the religions that lie east of Byzantium, but the most intriguing is yours. And your people's zeal, stretching out over centuries—more than a millennium— is quite impressive. I am keenly interested. What's more, there is now a rumor of a Messiah. But come, join me and my daughter in the banquet hall, along with my other guests. Then I shall hear from you, if you will, for I am particularly interested in the vision I have heard about. It was near Damascus, was it not?"

As the meal progressed, a few cold but civil words passed between Saul and Simon the scoundrel. But most of Saul's time was spent conversing with the daughter of Sergius Paulus. There was no doubt she had heard much of the Lord Jesus and was sincere about her interest in him.

When the festivities ended, the proconsul and his guests moved to the *oecus*, a large sitting room overlooking the sea. Again Sergius Paulus commanded the moment. "Saul, your name means 'great' or 'large' in your native tongue, does it not? In my language *Paulus* means 'small.' Perhaps, considering our stature, we should exchange names." Everyone laughed appreciatively, for the proconsul was a tall man, while Saul was not.

Saul surprised everyone with his response. "An excellent proposal, at least for me. I am no longer in the world of my own race. There are few Jews where I hope to go. Why not take a Roman name! I have been considering just such a thing. With your permission, Your Excellency, I shall take your advice—and your name."

Sergius Paulus showed sincere pleasure in Saul's words. "I had no idea you would take me seriously," he responded. "But by all means, take my name. I would be honored. And shall I take the name Saul?"

"Not if you wish to stay in good standing with the emperor," came the apostle's quick and mischievous reply.

"A wit worthy of a Roman, Paul of Tarsus," retorted Paulus. With those words spoken, everyone applauded.

"Now, to the purpose of this gathering. Paul, I am told by my friend Kala that you claim to have seen in a vision, or something of that sort, a man who rose from the dead. Will you not tell us of this event?"

As Paul stood, Simon Elymas Bar-Jesus yawned and stretched. Looking bored, he let everyone know by his demeanor that he would *tolerate* hearing from someone who was obviously his inferior.

Paul began with a brief description of his childhood, his training in Jerusalem, his having heard the rumors of the resurrection of Jesus, and his persecuting of the Way. "Many were beaten. Kala, your faithful servant, was in Jerusalem at the time. I ordered him imprisoned because of his faith. He refused to renounce his beliefs and was beaten."

Kala nodded. Simon was growing visibly nervous.

"On the road leading from Jerusalem to Damascus, I saw a great light. The light was Jesus, the Messiah, the only begotten Son of God, whom I saw standing before me—the very one I was persecuting. He told me that I would proclaim him to the Gentiles. Then I was struck blind and led to Damascus, where I took lodging. Then—"

Simon exploded. "Listen no more, Your Excellency. His words are but a fable. Jesus was a teacher, as I have told you, but no more. And this tale about being blinded is . . ."

Paul flashed. Pointing straight at Simon, he roared, "You son of the Devil, full of every sort of trickery and villainy, enemy of all that is good, will you never stop perverting the true ways of the Lord? And now the Lord has laid his hand of punishment upon you, and it is you who will be stricken with blindness."

For an instant Simon sneered. Then he trembled as fear engulfed him. Frantically passing his hands before his face, he cried, "No, no! It's getting dark! Help me! I can't see! Have mercy on me—I've gone blind!"

Simon then screamed, clutched his eyes, and fell to his knees, begging someone to lead him to Paul. Half-mad with fear, he screamed again and began pouring out confessions of wickedness and deceit that shocked everyone. Several servants and soldiers then led Simon out of the room, even as he begged to speak to Paul.

Sergius Paulus stood. "I believe, Paul of Tarsus. Dare I do any other? Your Lord is now my Lord."

The proconsul's daughter rushed to his side and began weeping. "Father, please, may I too believe and join you in your faith?"

∞

That evening Sergius Paulus was baptized, and it was that event that settled for Paul and Barnabas what they were to do. The believers who met at the assembly in New Paphos refused to allow Sergius Paulus, the very proconsul of Cyprus, to come into their assembly. They finally relented, but only if he would consent to be circumcised.

Paul was furious. Barnabas was dismayed. The next day, alone in their room, Paul confronted Barnabas. "It is your homeland, and I understand your feelings. I have the same deep longing for Tarsus. I am eager for the good news about Jesus to be preached in my home city. I desire to see my friends and their families follow the Lord, just as you do. But face it, Barnabas. The entire population of Jews on this island numbers only a thousand. All of them have already heard. Some, perhaps *all* who will ever believe, have *already* believed! There is no more to do here. You could spend a lifetime on Cyprus and nothing would change."

"I agree," Barnabas replied. Then he confessed, "One more meeting in one of those buildings, and I . . ."

Paul, still intent, continued. "These people do not even know there are Gentiles on this island. Look at their attitude toward Sergius Paulus. They demand that a proconsul of Rome be circumcised. Someday I plan to deliver the gospel of the Lord to the emperor Claudius. Shall I tell him he must be circumcised?"

Barnabas started to reply, but Paul interrupted again. "Do you remember that meeting in Antioch? We met before the

Lord and ministered to him. That day the Lord spoke to five men, separating two of us for a special ministry. To do what?"

Barnabas chuckled and raised his hands in a gesture of defeat. "Saul—or is it Paul? You really do intend to change your name, don't you? All right. Brother Paul, I am as ready as you are to leave this island. Let us go to places where the name of Jesus Christ has not been heard. And let us hope that in *that* place we find uncircumcised heathen to whom we can proclaim Jesus Christ."

"Do you know where such a place is?"

"I do!"

Paul was taken aback by so quick a response from his friend.

"The farthest known gathering of believers is northwest of here, three days by ship. Perhaps two days in good weather."

"What city?"

"Perga. A small seaport in the province of Pamphylia, up in Asia Minor. I am told there are eight believers there, all Jewish. Dear, dear people I am told. Beyond Perga, *nothing*. No assembly in any city! No one has ever heard of our Lord north of that point."

"Do you mean in Galatia?"

"Yes, the province of Galatia, in southeast Asia Minor."

"Good!" exclaimed a contented Paul. "Let us find the departure date of the next—"

"There is a ship loading its cargo now. I have already alerted Mark. The ship sails in three or four days, perhaps sooner. It is the first ship to sail north since the winter ended."

"Where is Mark? Out giving away food?"

"No, not this time. He is receiving it! The holy ones here in Paphos have prepared all sorts of food for us, food that does not spoil easily."

"All this happened since we were with the proconsul?"

"Why not?" replied Barnabas, breaking into a wide grin. "After all, I was afraid you might become so attached to Cyprus you'd want to make it your home." Paul threw a sandal at Barnabas, and the two men laughed.

"Poor Mark," added Paul. "As our burden for Cyprus lightens, Mark's burden once more grows heavier."

"Now to sleep, Paul. We must rise early and go straight to the port—before dawn! It is possible the ship is leaving no later than sunup. It depends on cargo and weather."

CHAPTER 7

There will be no sailing today. Not in this ship. The freight is loaded, yes, and its cargo well secured, but the sailing season has only begun. No ship has left this harbor since last fall. My crew is waiting for a sign from the gods, an omen. A *good* omen. So am I."

"You have sailed at this time in previous years, have you not?" asked Barnabas.

"Yes, but spring came too early this year. Winter takes revenge on an early spring."

"We heard another captain say the same thing just recently," replied Paul.

"He was a wise seaman," said the captain as he looked out upon the sea. "It is the Etesian winds we all fear. There's not a seaman on this island but knows of a mate who died by those winds."

Paul searched Barnabas's face for an explanation. "They are winds that sometimes come during this season," Barnabas explained. "They blow in from the north and east. Any ship sailing into those winds faces disaster. Sometimes the waves become like giant walls. When those waves collapse on a ship, the ship is in grave danger. Few survive the worst of these storms. Nonetheless, it is rare to see such winds this late in the year."

"I've seen them this late in the year," retorted the captain. "And always in years with an early spring. We will wait right here until the gods give us a good sign to sail under." With that, the captain stalked away.

"How long might we have to wait?" Paul asked Barnabas.

"A day, a week. The longer they wait, the more willing the sailors are to believe they have seen a good sign. But the captain, despite his superstitions, is making a wise choice. This has always been an island of seafarers. These people respect the seasons and the seas. Even if this is April, all men fear the possibility of Etesian winds."

"Then we shall wait. In the meantime, I'll wander these docks to see if I can find anyone who needs my services. Perhaps some ship or sailor has something that needs to be mended."

"And I will bargain with the captain for our fare to Attalia, the seaport town near Perga. I will also inquire as to the possibility of our sleeping on the ship's deck tonight. We don't want to miss a sudden departure.

"John Mark, come with me. While the captain and I haggle over the price of passage to the province of Pamphylia, perhaps we can use some of that fine Hebrew food to get a reduced price."

"We could bargain with a dozen captains and still have food for a month," replied Mark, shaking his head as he stared at the two overstuffed bags at his feet.

That evening a spotted seagull landed on the bow of the ship. Had it been two, or if it had been anywhere except the bow, the incident would have gone unnoticed. But one spotted seagull, in the evening, on the ship's bow, was sign enough that the gods were telling the captain to set sail on the morrow.

The last of the deck cargo was loaded by morning's light.

As Barnabas and Paul waited on the pier, an old man approached them. "You sail on her?" the old man inquired in a cracked voice. Paul nodded. The old man searched the faces of the two men. "You are from this island?"

"I am from Tarsus, in the Taurus Mountains of Syria. My friend is from Antioch, but he once lived here, yes."

The old man stared at Barnabas. "You would sail into the Etesian winds?"

"They are blowing, sir?"

"Not blowing, not yet," said the old man, throwing one hand into the air. "But I feel them! I can tell. You cannot feel them, but they *are* blowing. Tomorrow they will blow harder, and there will be vengeance in them. No ship sailing north from this harbor will be able to stand against these winds. Listen to me. I have sailed these seas since I was a boy. I have fought those winds many a time, and never have I won. Few who have seen what I've seen have lived to tell the tale." The old man glared at Paul. "Never sail the Etesian winds. Remember my words: Never the Etesian winds!"

At that moment, slaves on the dock began moving along the ship's side, loosening the ropes that moored her to the dock. That done, the slaves began pushing on the ship's side with their poles.

"You may come aboard now," the captain shouted. "Quickly!"

For the second time in less than a month, three Hebrew men rushed aboard a freighter about to sail the Mediterranean. Unlike at Salamis, however, there was no man-made channel to the sea. This was the sea. The morning winds immediately caught the hoisted sail, and the ship slid peacefully into the calm waters.

"Never the Etesian winds!" the old man cried one last time.

The captain approached. "There will be no food or water provided for you. You can make your beds and sleep on the deck between the cargo. If the waters become too rough, or if it begins to rain, you will be allowed below. Otherwise . . ."

"Yes, we know," interrupted Mark. "We've sailed before."

Barnabas moved to the stern of the old freighter and stared back at the receding coast of Cyprus. "I'll return to this island if ever my people open themselves—and the churches—to the Gentiles," he said wistfully.

"Would it be of any great advantage?"

"What?" asked Barnabas, turning to face Paul.

"In the church in Antioch, during the four years of its existence, a few Jews have become believers. But have they found it easy to be part of an informal Gentile church?"

"No," replied a cautious Barnabas, already seeing that he had accidentally opened a very serious conversation.

"And did the Jews who came into the Antioch assembly try to change the Gentile expression of the bride of Christ?"

"Yes."

"Did they succeed?"

"No."

"And did some get deeply hurt?"

Barnabas was silent.

"Did the Gentiles change their cultural ways to satisfy the Jewish believers who came among them? Could they, even if they tried? No. They will always be Gentiles, not Jews. The *Gentile* way should prevail in an assembly of Gentiles gathering in a *Gentile* land.

"Now reverse that," Paul continued. "The churches on Cyprus are Jewish, Hebrew to the core. If Gentiles were to come to the meetings of these Jewish churches—even if they eventually outnumbered the Jews—they would still be in a Jewish experience of the body of Christ, would they not?"

Barnabas sighed, knowing every word was true.

"Look at Israel. Look at the people who fled Jerusalem. When I was trying to destroy the assembly in Jerusalem, what did the people do who fled? Moving out into the towns and villages of Judea, they took the ways of the Jerusalem church with them. They were Hebrews in a Hebrew land with a Hebrew culture, fleeing into Hebrew towns and villages. The result? The churches in all those towns look exactly like miniature copies of the ecclesias they came from. They all look like the Jerusalem assembly.

"Anyway, even if Gentiles were to be accepted in the Cyprus churches, those churches will *never* be Gentile churches. That's the way it is. That's the way it will always be.

"But if a church is planted far enough away, with no other churches nearby to influence it, and if a renegade starts that church . . ."

"You are referring to Antioch?" said Barnabas with a smile, knowing that the gathering there was *very* Gentile and *very* free and that he himself was regarded as a renegade by some of the believers in Jerusalem.

"My dear Barnabas, even to this day we don't know if the church in Jerusalem accepts Antioch as a *real* gathering. It's not Jewish, you know."

"We will never know until Peter comes. That's just the way Jerusalem is. *Peter* will decide."

"I don't like that. *God* knows it is an assembly. And the people are his, even if their culture isn't Jewish. But for your sake, Barnabas, the longer Peter stays in Jerusalem, the better for you and for the ecclesia in Jerusalem. You are the one who broke ranks and allowed Gentiles to be saved—and not just to be saved but to assemble as the body of Christ."

Barnabas shivered in the wind. "It could be a dark day for me if Peter goes to Antioch. Peter is my father in Christ, you know."

"Or it might be a most glorious day."

"That is my hope."

"If Peter sides with the Pharisees, there will never be true Gentile churches," Paul responded quietly. "And yes, *that* will be the darkest of all days."

"But right now we're on our way to some obscure place called Pamphylia to raise up a Gentile church. That will *surely* make Jerusalem love us!"

"You mean we're in even worse trouble with Jerusalem because of our going to Galatia?"

"Yes! Especially since Jerusalem Pharisees have begun receiving the Lord's life and are joining the assembly there. This is a new thing, Pharisees in the ecclesia. It could make the Jerusalem church very legalistic. I have heard that even Blastinius counts himself a follower of the Lord."

"Blastinius!" Paul was aghast. "No, not Blastinius. That man would make Abraham quote all 633 laws of Moses before he would shake hands with him."

"An unlikely convert, Paul?"

"Yes," replied Paul emphatically.

"Know any other unlikely converts?"

Paul chuckled. "I am as skeptical of Blastinius as your people on Cyprus were of me."

There was a long silence. A cold wind blew across the ship. "It's getting cold. Let's find a warmer place between some of the cargo."

"The Etesian winds?"

"I hope not. This conversation is gloom enough for me. But, Paul, despite all you have said, I confess that I still hold out hope for Cyprus."

"I suppose it is good that one of us does. I belong out there, Barnabas—out where there are no believers."

The sea was calm for the rest of the day, but as night fell the wind rose, as did the waves. One phrase was now being muttered by all the seamen: "The Etesian winds!"

That night the captain ordered the three men off the deck and into the cargo hold. "Young man," the captain said sternly, "you'd better hold those sacks of food close to your chest."

Mark mistakenly thought the captain was referring to thieving sailors.

As the sea grew in violence, the three men moved to the center of the ship to prevent seasickness. The next morning Paul and Barnabas were awakened by the frantic scream of John Mark. "Rats! They've got rats down here as big as dogs. And they all want my food!"

"You can tie it to that twine hanging down from the ceiling or take it on deck," instructed one of the sailors. "Otherwise, give it to 'em."

Mark quickly climbed atop some of the cargo, reached up, and tied his two bags to a rope dangling from the overhead rafters.

"Will that stop them?"

"No, but you can see them better as they make their way down the rope. Then you hit them with a stick."

"Hit the rats!" he exclaimed in panic. "What if they fall on me?!"

"They often do," answered the sailor with a smirk.

Mark again climbed on top of the cargo and retrieved his satchels. "I'll take them on deck. I'll find a dry place up there somewhere. Even rats aren't going to be out in this kind of weather."

What met Mark's eyes struck terror into his heart. The sea had become watery hills, reaching as high as the ship's mast. The sailors on deck were frantically trying to tie down loose cargo. "The cargo will rip right through the side railings if it breaks loose," he heard one say.

"She'll be listing before night," predicted another.

"There won't be a mother's son alive by morning," cried another.

"Where can I put these?" yelled Mark.

"Stuff them between the cargo, and go below before you get

yourself killed. Better you wait for the sea to kill you than it be your own doing."

Mark stuffed the bags of food under some of the cargo. The bag containing the scrolls was still below, as was Paul's bag of tools. As Mark staggered down the ladder, he called out to Barnabas, "It's terrible out there."

"The sea—is it waves or swells?" asked Barnabas, his face intense.

"Uh, swells, I guess."

"How high?"

"As high as the railing; a few even higher and getting higher still."

Barnabas slipped back against the cargo. "It's an Etesian storm!"

"Oh no," moaned Mark. "That's what the sailors said."

"So late for a winter storm. But this ship is too small for the fury of winter weather. If she takes the full brunt of such a storm, she's not likely to stay afloat."

"What do we do?" asked Paul.

"Perhaps the only thing we can do . . . *die.*"

Though it was only early evening, it was already as dark as midnight. Soon rain was falling in torrents. The sailors cut the sails away and dropped anchor. The whole crew took refuge in the cargo hold. Men and ship were at the mercy of a merciless sea. The swells had grown to heights higher than the ship's mast.

By afternoon of the next day, the storm had unleashed its full fury on the battered ship. Suddenly a wave swelled, lifting the ship high into the air. As the ship began sliding down the swell, it slipped over onto its side. The deck cargo ripped loose and tore the railing off the starboard side as it plunged into the sea. Cargo in the hold broke loose and began tumbling to the starboard side.

"The cargo's shifted! She'll sink for sure," cried the captain.

"Every seaman to the deck! Lash yourself to something. Take ropes and hooks with you. Four of us—the tallest ones—will remain below. We'll hand as much cargo as we can to those above."

"My tools, Barnabas. Save them if you can. Mark, come with me," ordered Paul. Just before stepping out onto the deck, Paul turned and shouted back to Barnabas, "Whoever survives goes to the Gentiles. *No turning back!*"

Looking out at the listing ship, Mark and Paul knew instantly that the ship was now a tomb. With the side railing gone, nothing stood between men and the sea. Everyone on deck began tying ropes around their waists and lashing the other ends to the center mast.

"Over here," called a seaman. The sailors had pulled back the covering to the cargo bay. Men below began throwing ropes up. "Pull!" those below shouted. "When the cargo reaches the deck, push it overboard."

As Paul struggled with the other men to lift a heavy load out of the belly of the ship, he caught a glimpse of Barnabas. He tried to speak, but the howling wind had ended all hope of communication.

When a giant swell collapsed over the deck, the ship momentarily disappeared below the surface of the sea. When at last it struggled back to the surface, several men were missing. The ship now listed hard to the right. The storm continued its rage against the ship that had dared to sail its winter seas.

Mark and Paul, struggling to maintain their balance on the steeply tilted deck, were standing near a teak cabinet when a giant wave engulfed the ship. Paul felt an excruciating pain around his waist. The rope choking his waist broke, and he was washed into the hungry sea. Surfacing, he gasped for air and looked around. Mark was also in the water.

"Grab hold of the cabinet, Mark," cried Paul.

Paul swam toward a small chest, hoping it could help him stay above water.

Barnabas scrambled to the deck. It was void of men.

"Gone. Lost to the gods of winter," said the captain as he peered out.

At that moment lightning flashed. For a brief instant the sea was lit as bright as day.

"Look!" cried a seaman. "There's another ship out there."

"It's Roman. A grain ship. She's the only kind of ship plying the seas that might survive this night."

"Lamps to the deck!" shouted the captain. "They won't burn long, but perhaps the other ship will see us. Lamps to the deck," he called again.

By morning the storm had emptied its wrath. The freighter, virtually submerged, lay on its side in a calm sea. Everyone clinging to the derelict breathed silent relief as the huge Roman ship began making its way toward the wreckage. Boats were lowered. Soon seamen from the grain ship were rowing alongside the wreckage. Scattered across the seascape were men hanging desperately to pieces of wreckage and floating cargo. Those with any strength began swimming toward the saving ship. One by one they were lifted aboard. One such man was Barnabas, a satchel still slung over his shoulder.

For hours those on board and those in the longboats searched for survivors. "There is no one left," the two captains finally agreed. The boats were called back. The grain ship hoisted its sails and began to slide through the wreckage.

"There!" shouted Barnabas. "I see a man's head."

"There are three of them!"

Sure enough, three or four sailors had pulled several wooden cabinets together and had managed to hang on to them all night long.

"There's another man out here," one of the survivors cried out.

It was Paul, holding tenaciously to a cabinet. A rope was lowered and then tied around Paul's waist. When he failed to respond, his limp body was pulled up the side of the ship. His face was so swollen Barnabas recognized him only by his clothes. "Is Mark out there?" Barnabas asked desperately.

Paul gave no answer.

"Fill him with fresh water, then force it out of him. It may kill him, but he's dead anyway," a sailor called out.

"If he gains consciousness, take him to my cabin," said the ship's captain.

Barnabas was amazed at the captain's words. The other survivors had all been taken below. "Why?" he asked, turning his haggard face toward the captain.

The captain pointed to the leather cord around Paul's neck. "Like me, that man is a citizen of Rome. We take care of our own."

There was another loud cry. "I see one more!" Barnabas ran to the railing.

"He's dead; leave him in the sea," someone said.

"Maybe not. He managed to tie himself to a piece of the mast."

"He's dead, I tell you."

"That's my nephew! Pull him up," commanded Barnabas with a growl. "A dead man doesn't straddle a mast."

One last time a boat was lowered. "Tie his legs together and lift him up to me feet first," Barnabas shouted again.

Mark's body was lifted onto the deck, his head dangling downward. On the way up, he coughed. Barnabas reached out and grabbed Mark's feet, then pulled the young man on board, still holding him by his feet. Using every bit of his great strength, he lifted Mark's feet above his own head and began shaking him furiously. "On the authority of our Lord, I tell you, John Mark, *breathe!*" roared Barnabas.

Salt water began pouring out of Mark's mouth. He coughed

again. Barnabas, still holding Mark's feet above his head, con-tinued shaking his nephew and bellowing, "Breathe!" Mark gasped for air.

Still holding Mark's feet, Barnabas then began swinging him around in a circle. More water poured out of him. Barnabas swung Mark in an ever faster circle, shouting, "Breathe! Breathe!" An amazed audience of heathen seamen looked on in disbelief.

As Barnabas continued to swing him, Mark began to gasp for air. For an instant Barnabas let Mark lie on the deck, then he gathered his nephew into his arms and headed for the captain's quarters.

"Is he a Roman?" asked one of the crew.

"No," rumbled Barnabas. "He's the son of a King."

Barnabas wrapped Paul and John Mark tightly in the heavi-est cloth he could find on board, then ordered the room to be heated. After that he continually dampened both men's mouths with fresh water.

Some hours later, Paul awoke, burning with fever. "Barna-bas?"

"Yes. You're alive! Paul! You who love the Gentiles so much were rescued by them. You are in the captain's own room on a grain ship. God has kept you to fulfill your call."

"Barnabas," Paul whispered again. Barnabas leaned down to hear his friend's faint words. "Never again the Etesian winds!"

Shortly thereafter John Mark awoke, coughing wildly. See-ing Barnabas, he smiled and whispered, "At least I got rid of the lice."

Barnabas laughed, then added, "I have more good news, Mark. I managed to rescue all of our clothing, the scrolls, and Paul's tools. But we lost both your satchels of food." Mark smiled again, then drifted back to sleep.

Paul motioned to Barnabas. "Where are we?"

"We are headed for Attalia, the port city of Pamphylia. It is only seven miles down from Perga. We will dock by morning. Just as soon as we do, I will find lodging, then a doctor."

Three times
I was shipwrecked.
Once I spent a whole night
and a day
adrift at sea.

CHAPTER 8

Youth is with him. He'll live," said the doctor. "There's salt water in his lungs, but the fever should burn that out after a few days."

"Now, that one over there, that's a different story. First, his back is infected. How in the name of the gods did he come to be covered with so many open wounds? That alone is enough. He, too, has water in his lungs. If he recovers, it will take him longer. I'd not move him if I were you. Leave him to rest until he's wholly well. I'm leaving medicine for both; but more, I leave them to the gods. You say you have friends here in Pamphylia?"

"Yes," replied Barnabas, "in your capital city, Perga. But I have not yet contacted them."

"You will need them; at least these two will need them. For the next few weeks it could go either way for your friend with . . . with the whipped back. Don't move him from this inn for some time. By the way, I've seen these lashes before. When you Jews disagree about your teachings, you have no limits, do you?"

Paul laughed. The doctor smiled. "He hasn't lost his humor. He'll need it."

After the doctor departed, Paul raised his head. "Don't let

the believers know we are here. Not yet. You know the mind of the Jews. If a man is ill, it means God is punishing him."

Barnabas's brow wrinkled. "When we do meet them, how shall I explain our being here so long without contacting them? Besides, I'm not sure being shipwrecked falls into the category of sickness, even for the most religious Jews. Anyway, my dear brother, these holy ones in Perga are not just Jews. They are also your brothers and sisters in Christ."

Paul sank back into the matted straw. "I hope you're right. I don't look forward to being lectured on how wantonly evil I must be because I am sick."

"Oh, they won't do that," replied Barnabas cheerily. "They'll just condemn you for not having enough faith!"

Paul's laugh turned into a series of painful coughs.

The next evening the small room where Paul and Mark lay recovering was visited by the sisters and brothers from Perga. Barnabas had followed his own counsel. For the next two weeks those loving believers in Perga cared for Paul and Mark as though they had nothing else in all the world to do.

"They are as beautiful in Christ as we had been told," observed Paul.

In the days to come Barnabas spent much of his free time with one of the brothers, Ahira, a giant of a man. They had met in Jerusalem at Pentecost some seventeen years before. Ahira told him how a group of Jewish believers had come to exist in Perga of Pamphylia. Ahira was a merchant who derived his livelihood by buying and selling goods brought by sea to the Attalia harbor. He also traded in goods that were floated down the Cestrus River, which flowed into Perga from the north. It turned out that Ahira also knew a great deal about the land that lay north of them.

"We are the only believers in this part of the world. I know there are none beyond here, for I have traveled the Augustan Road to Galatia many times. I go there in July."

"This is April," observed Barnabas. "We can't wait till July."

"Never in April. Brigands fill the mountains this time of year. You should wait until later," he counseled. Then he added, "But as of now, it is time to move Paul and Mark to my home. They should be able to make the seven-mile trip to my house. When you come, each of you will have a separate room."

Ahira and his family moved out of their home and into the home of another family in the assembly, thereby leaving the whole house to the three brothers. And the Lord's dear people in Perga looked upon Paul's ordeal not as punishment but as a miracle of the Lord's mercy.

After two weeks had passed, Paul and Mark were able to move about, though both continued to cough blood. Every afternoon Mark came down with a fever that lasted about two hours. Paul's greater pain was his back, where infection persisted. For both men, strength returned slowly.

One morning Mark awoke with a burning fever. "A relapse," he moaned. "I don't think I'll ever recover." A sense of hopelessness had enveloped him.

That afternoon, still burning with fever, Mark made his way to the living room where Barnabas and Paul were talking. "May I speak? I heard there is a ship leaving from Attalia tomorrow." Mark hesitated. "Its destination is Caesarea."

Paul's heart sank.

"It can take me to Israel inside a week. Brothers, I must go home. I think I'm dying. Maybe not, but I'm no use to either of you."

The two apostles sat stunned. Neither spoke.

"Uncle, you must let me go."

Paul was not angry with Mark, but he was sorry to hear his request. Finally, he and Barnabas capitulated to Mark's desires, though they desperately needed him. What coursed through Paul's mind, however, was concern for what it would do to

Mark's inner man if he turned back. Paul feared that Mark would never trust himself again if he returned to Jerusalem.

Barnabas thought first of the problems Mark's leaving would create. Then he wondered how his sister would feel about Mark's giving up. He spoke one final word to Mark. "Are you sure?"

"Yes. I can't go on."

"It will be difficult, almost impossible, to continue on without you, Mark," Paul said quietly.

Mark dropped his eyes.

"Do as you feel you should," Paul added. "But tell me, how will you get from Caesarea to Jerusalem?"

"We have close kin in Caesarea," answered Barnabas.

"We will go with you to the port, Mark."

"Thank you, Paul."

An hour later two older men laid hands on a younger man, prayed for him, and sent him on his way back to his homeland.

"Mark's passage took a large part of our money," said Barnabas as the two men returned to Ahira's house. "We will have to be very careful with what we have left until we reach a city where we can ply our respective trades."

"Yes," answered Paul reflectively. "And because we must now carry all our luggage, we will not be able to carry much food. So we will have to be careful with both money and food."

"He is young, Paul. He will grow."

"One thing is for sure—he belongs in Israel and not out here," observed Paul.

"That may be, but we're going to miss his help," said Barnabas as he looked northward at the road leading out of Perga.

CHAPTER 9

It is the wildest, most dangerous strip of road in the empire,"
said Ahira. "Even the might of Rome cannot tame it," added
another brother. The four brothers who lived in Perga had
gathered in Ahira's home to counsel Barnabas and Paul and pray
with them concerning their journey northward.

"The Augustan Road. It was built by Rome. That is, by
slaves. It slopes upward, and the plateau you finally reach is four
thousand feet higher than here. Only now have a few people
begun to travel north. Until now it has been impassable from
winter's snow. You would be wise to wait until Roman garrisons
begin passing back and forth to Galatia."

"We have prayed for guidance and believe we should go
now," the two men responded in agreement.

"Then try never to travel alone."

"Are there inns or way stations?"

"Yes, but not all are open, not yet. In fact, very few are open
this time of year. Winter may not be over; winter often takes
revenge on an early spring."

"Yes, we have heard the saying several times now," responded Barnabas.

"But robbers are not your only concern, nor is cold
weather."

"What, then?"

"The flooding. Unexpected, unpredictable floods pouring down out of nowhere. These floods are legendary. They've drowned many a man walking along the road. The flooding waters use the road as a riverbed, sweeping people to their death in an instant."

Ahira paused, then said, "One more thing."

"Oh no." Paul grimaced.

"Ahira, please, a positive word," Barnabas said.

"Ice and snow are just now melting, so even if there are no floods, the rivers will be swollen; some of those rivers may prove to be impassable. So remember, travel with others.

"Also, after a day's journey from here, you must always travel at night. Even then, travel in utter silence. The thieves and robbers have hiding places all along the road. Furthermore, when you come to an inn or a way station, unless there are Roman soldiers there, do not go in. Robbers often attack the way stations this time of year. They beat, rob, and kidnap. They have even been known to kill. What you must do, therefore, is find someplace in the forest that is thick and dry. Sleep there during the day. And if you do stay at an inn, soldiers or not, remember that thieves are always present."

Ahira drew in his breath. "About these robbers. They have gone all winter without victims. They are hungry, and that makes them bold. That is what makes this season the most dangerous time of the year to travel."

"When they lay hold of someone, what do they usually do?"

"Usually they take everything, including clothes. Sometimes they keep their victims for a while before letting them go. Most travelers, of course, have little or no money on them. If you have money, they beat you for being rich. If you have none, they beat you for having none. Either way you are beaten! I warn you, brothers, *some* they kill. They are hungry and daring. And Rome is traveling this route very little."

Paul sighed.

"The shipwreck doesn't look so bad after all," said Barnabas.

"I repeat, travel at night, hide during the day, utter not a word. Never sleep on the road nor near it. Seek high ground. If you hear a roar that sounds like rushing water, get off the road and run for higher ground!"

"What is the first city we will come to?"

"Just after you reach the plateau, you will come to a Roman city. Very Roman. They say the square—or I should say, squares—look just like the forums of Rome. The name of the town is Antioch of Pisidia."

"Antioch! We left one Antioch, and now we head for another Antioch. But it is not surprising. I've heard there are sixteen cities in the empire named Antioch."

"Actually, the name of the city is an error. It sits about a mile outside the province of Pisidia. But no one seems to consider that. For all practical purposes, you are in the province of Pisidia when you arrive in Antioch," observed Ahira.

"Now, are you sure you don't want to wait for a military escort or at least until there is a caravan?"

"When will that be?"

"No one knows. A week, a month. Meanwhile, you could stay and help us here in Perga."

"You have grown dear to us," replied Paul. "Your care for us will forever be remembered."

"And your love for us and for one another—well, we have seen nothing to compare, not since leaving home," added Barnabas.

"But?"

"There are ten Jews in Perga, and eight of you are believers, thank God! In fact, half are in this room right now! In Antioch—uh, Antioch of Syria, not Antioch of Pisidia—our Lord sent us out to go to the Gentiles. There are thousands of

Gentiles in Antioch of Pisidia. And none of them in all that city, not *one* of them, has ever heard of the Lord Jesus."

"We have decided to wait no longer to do what God has sent us to do," added Paul. "With your permission and your prayers, we will depart for the Galatian plateau tomorrow."

"Then we must prepare food for you, food that will not spoil. We can . . ."

"Only enough for one or two days, please. We must travel very light. Mark came with us to be our baggage carrier, but in his absence, two men must do the work of three."

"We will all go a day's journey with you—all eight of us. At that point we will bid you good-bye and leave you to the care of our Lord," said Ahira.

The next morning before dawn, eight dear saints, who had already helped our three brothers so very much, laid aside their day's work and walked with the two men until late afternoon.

"You will be safe tonight. There are even places along the way where you might be received as a guest, for a price. But tomorrow you will see no more houses along the road. No one dares live in sight of the road—not until you reach Antioch of Pisidia.

"One more word. It's about the Galatian region. You know that over half of all the people in the empire are slaves. In Galatia it is more like eight out of ten are slaves. Beyond that, the poor are very poor. The towns and villages are especially poor. And because most people are slaves, you will find virtually no one who can read or write. Keep these things in mind as you proclaim Christ. Those few who can read, and the even fewer who can write, will be Greek and Hebrew merchants."

"Are there many freed men?" asked Paul.

"Slaves made free? Yes, a few freed men, but far less than you find in most places. A race of people called Phrygians makes up the largest group of people in Galatia. The word *Phrygian*, as you know, means "slave" in Latin. They are literally a race enslaved. Consequently, few of them are ever set free by their owners. In fact, few wish to be free. In general *freed* men in Galatia live a far harsher life than do slaves.

"Brother Paul, you will find it difficult to make a living in Galatia. There are so many slaves, they dominate the market-place. They always underbid other artisans. You will be blessed, indeed, the day you earn a denarius."

"Oh, do they use coins?"

"Well, most people, as in all the empire, have never seen a coin—or at least never use them. Almost everything is done by bartering."

"Then I will not work for denarii. I will barter for my labor."

"Can you barter for less than a slave can barter for?"

"No, I cannot. Which means I will starve . . . unless some-one is seeking the best quality of workmanship within my trade."

"It is time to say good-bye. It should take you from five to ten days to reach the plateau, depending on the weather."

"Brothers and sisters, your love and care for us have been from the Lord himself," said Barnabas.

"You are brave men," said Ahira. "Now let us all gather around our two madmen and ask the Lord to keep them safe."

So they prayed. And embraced. And sang a song. And said good-bye.

And so it came to pass, in the sixth year of the reign of the emperor Claudius, that two apostles—sent ones—departed the farthest place on earth where believers in Christ were known to exist. They marched off the map into a Gentile world where Christ's name had never been heard. They would soon plant churches among uncircumcised heathen—churches unlike any-thing ever seen before.

But not before both men were almost killed, *several* times!

CHAPTER 10

Mile fifteen, according to that Roman marker," said Paul as he pointed to a stone pillar beside the road.

"This is where we should start sleeping in the day," Barnabas responded. "This is probably safe territory, but I don't want to take the risk that it might not be. Let's wait until midnight, then walk until daybreak. We may not sleep today, but tomorrow we'll be so exhausted that we'll surely sleep then."

The two men walked deep into the woods until the underbrush made it impossible to go farther. Paul took the first watch, knowing he would find it difficult to sleep.

When the deepest of night finally came, they quietly slipped back onto the road. Just before sunrise they saw the lights of an inn, with chariots of Rome harnessed nearby. "I hope they don't need new harnesses," Barnabas muttered as they entered the courtyard.

"I'll gladly give them free harnesses if they are headed north."

Unfortunately, the soldiers were headed south. And the two men's stay in that inn proved to be the last safe place they would know until Galatia. When evening came, they paid their bill and took to the road again, assured by the innkeeper that there had been no reports of robbers so far. "Of course, we've only been open two days," he added.

In a night as black as death, the two men walked as fast as endurance would allow. Every strange sound, every shadow, put them on edge. The alarm that gripped them when a dog crossed the road made them realize how fearful was the night. Just before dawn they again edged their way into the forest. Pulling bushes and shrubs, sticks and leaves about them, they lay down and remained motionless until the midnight watch again cloaked them in safety.

The road was steep now, and a steady trickle of cold water flowed down the road, making them remember that winter snow was still melting and floods were still possible. Their feet soon grew numb from walking through the icy water. At last they stopped to rest, both men suffering from leg cramps. A cold mist had blown through the forest all night, leaving it almost impossible to find a dry place to lie down. Nonetheless, they crawled into their leather coats, sat under a tree dripping water, and slept fitfully.

"We have come about the distance that a horse can travel in one day. That means there must be an inn not far ahead."

Barnabas was right. There was an inn, and the innkeeper told them of a northbound caravan due to arrive soon. Two other travelers were staying at the inn—one a Greek merchant, the other a slave trader on his way to buy slaves in the market-place of Antioch of Pisidia.

"Will there be guards with the caravan?" Paul asked the innkeeper.

"No, not likely. Furthermore, it's a poor decision, if you ask me, for a caravan to be going this early. It's not bravery; it's stupidity. Better for an unguarded caravan to travel in the summer when the robbers' bellies are full."

"Then we will not wait for the caravan," responded Barnabas.

"These are our plans also," responded one of the Greeks.

"Shall we go together?" Paul and Barnabas eyed the two barbarians closely, finally concluding that not even the best of robbers could imitate Greek merchants.

"As you wish. Perhaps four will be a bit safer. But frankly, I wish you both carried a Roman sword and rode a steed!" Barnabas replied with a smile.

That evening the four men set their feet on the northern slopes of the Roman road. But it was far too early, Paul felt, and the two barbarians were talking much too loudly. "I think we made a poor choice for traveling companions," Paul whispered to Barnabas.

Just before dawn the four men left the road and began climbing a nearby hill, searching for high ground. But in this higher altitude the trees had thinned, no longer providing them the thick protection they needed. The men finally settled into a small grove of trees about halfway up the hill, pulling as much underbrush around them as possible.

After a few moments Barnabas whispered to Paul, "This isn't good. We need a safer place." With gestures to convey their intentions to their traveling companions, Barnabas and Paul climbed to the top of the hill. After a long search, they decided to crawl under a large overhanging boulder. Scooping out dirt with their hands, they managed to create enough space under the rock to slip in.

A few hours later the two men were awakened by screams. Bandits had found the Greeks. The two apostles watched in horror as they saw a band of robbers beat their two victims, strip them naked, then drag them down the side of the hill, feet first.

"That could be us right now," whispered Paul.

"I think they know we are around here somewhere. They'll be back looking for us. Leave your satchel in this hole. We must run; and we must run fast, hard, and far," replied Barnabas.

The two men crawled out from under the boulder, rammed

their satchels deep into the hole, then ran as far and as fast as strength allowed.

It began to rain. Using the weather as cover, they worked their way back to the boulder after nightfall, removed their bags, returned to the road, and walked until the first light of day.

"What's that?" cried Barnabas.

"Listen," exclaimed Paul. "Water!"

The two men scrambled up the embankment beside the road. As they did, a wall of water higher than Paul's head came hurtling toward them, turning the road into a river. They stared in silent amazement at the fury of this deluge that had come from nowhere.

"A moment later and we would have been on our way back to Perga!" said Paul soberly.

"And fully baptized," responded Barnabas in his best humor.

"There's good in this, Barnabas."

"Please be quick to share it."

"As long as this road is flooded, we are safe from robbers. When the water subsides, let's go back down to the road. A little wading won't hurt us."

Barnabas mulled over the idea. "You're right. Only fools and Christians would be out in this weather."

"We are good candidates for both," retorted Paul dryly. "Anyway, I'd rather be drowned than beaten to death."

The waters eventually sank to ankle deep, allowing the men to travel for two days in broad daylight. But at the end of those two days they were exhausted, and their food was almost gone. Worse, the weather was once more turning wintry.

"The longest winter I've ever experienced," commented Barnabas as the evening brought on howling winds and traces of snow.

"If we're going to survive this night, we'd better keep walking," said Paul. Wrapped in their water-soaked leather coats, the two men staggered up the sloppy road, often stumbling into the cold waters.

"Safety soon," said Barnabas, not knowing that the worst of all was just ahead.

> I have faced danger
> from flooded rivers
> and from robbers.
> I have lived with weariness
> and pain
> and sleepless nights.

CHAPTER 11

If that Roman marker is correct, we are, thank God, only three miles from Antioch. If Ahira is right, there should be an inn not too far distant."

Weak, hungry, and on the verge of collapse, the two men trudged forward.

"There's a river ahead. I can hear it," said Barnabas. "It must be one of the tributaries of the Anthius River. We are near the Pisidian border. That means there's shelter beyond this river—if we don't freeze first."

Then the worst of all possible sights came into view. The bridge across the river was completely washed away. There could be no crossing.

"We're stranded!" choked Barnabas.

"Look!" exclaimed Paul.

Someone, probably Roman soldiers, had strung a rope across the river, anchoring it on each side of the water. About halfway across, the rope was submerged.

"That rope is our only hope of survival, Paul. We've got to pull ourselves across or die." Paul nodded in agreement. "If we want to have dry clothes when we get to the other side, we'll have to strip now and carry our clothes across in our satchels. Paul, you go first. You carry the satchel that has your tools.

You'll have to pull yourself across hand over hand, but never let go of the rope; if you do, you will be swept under by the current. I'll cross as soon as you are on the other side. I'll carry the bag with our clothes in it. And I'll do my best to keep it out of the water so we have something dry to put on when we get across."

Paul quickly disrobed, rolled up his clothes, stuffed them deep into the bag, and then placed the wax-covered scrolls on top of them. He then grabbed the rope, slipped into the icy torrent, and began pulling his way across, hand over hand. He almost immediately lost his footing, but with a firm grip still on the rope, he managed to work his way to the middle of the river. As the rope emerged into view, Paul called, "The rope is frayed. It's about to break." He frantically reached out to get one hand beyond the fray. Just then the rope broke, and Paul was swung to the other side.

In a moment Paul had pulled himself up onto the bank, looked back helplessly at Barnabas, then crawled over to a tree, naked and freezing. He looked again at Barnabas. No words were needed. The two men were on opposite sides of a swollen river, with no possible way for either one to cross over to the other. Unless something happened quickly, Paul would soon be dead.

> Often
> I have shivered with cold,
> without enough clothing
> to keep me warm.

Instantly, Barnabas darted down the riverbank in search of a place he could forge. An hour passed before he reached Paul's side. Paul was unconscious in the snow, his body blue and shaking violently. Barnabas scooped Paul into his arms and began running as fast as he could, looking in every direction for shelter of any kind. Shortly he spotted an empty goat shed. Entering it, he wrapped Paul in all the dry clothing in the bag.

Nonetheless, Barnabas knew Paul's needs were far beyond such meager help. He wrapped both leather coats around Paul and once more took him in his arms and began running in the direction of Antioch of Pisidia.

An inn came into view. Barnabas burst through the door. "I have a dying man here," he shouted to the startled innkeeper. "Move away from the fireplace, everyone. Quick, find dry clothes. Anything! As long as it is dry."

Barnabas lay Paul's body as near the fire as he dared while others, speechless, scurried for dry clothing. "Innkeeper! Do you have a room?" called Barnabas without turning around.

"Yes!"

"Is it clean?"

"No. We are only just now opening, and we have not had time . . ."

"Burn it."

"What?"

"Burn it. Burn the room, now."

"That will cost you."

"Burn it now, do you hear?"

The innkeeper grabbed a bottle of wine and a torch, then rushed down the hall, darting into an empty room. He began pouring the alcohol on the filthy straw. He stared at the room for a moment, then threw the torch onto the straw and stepped back. A moment later the room was an inferno. Several rats rushed out; all else in the stone chamber was consumed.

"Now clean it! And fresh straw."

"It will cost you."

"Do it!" thundered Barnabas, still holding Paul before the fireplace.

When the room was finally cleaned, Barnabas gave one last command. "Everyone. Bring a torch and come with me. Stand in the room with your torches until the room is hot—unbearably hot."

Half a dozen torches were brought into the room. Covered by a pile of clothing and lying on fresh straw, Paul's shaking body began to calm.

"Get a doctor," Barnabas said.

"Your friend—he's a Jew, isn't he?"

"Yes, a Jew."

"Jew or Greek, with or without a doctor, he'll die. Besides, no doctor will come out here in this weather."

"God only takes devout Jews; this man keeps company with Gentiles. He'll live. Now find someone to get a doctor, and tell the doctor to come. But with or without a doctor, this man *will live.*"

It was not until the next morning that a doctor finally arrived. What he found was an emaciated patient. "This man has a severely infected back, a high fever, water in his lungs, and he's spitting blood. What do you expect me to do?"

"Everything," Barnabas said quietly.

"His back I can help. As to the rest of his condition, I see little hope. The man's strength has been ravaged. What has he been through—imprisonment? Starvation?"

"A shipwreck and the Augustan Road."

"The Augustan Road? Are you one of the survivors of the caravan?"

"What?" asked a confused Barnabas.

"An entire caravan was robbed and killed. At an inn. Their throats were slit."

"We heard that a caravan was coming, but we left before it arrived," replied Barnabas soberly.

"Two other bodies were found. Greek merchants, I believe."

"Yes, we were with them one night," responded Barnabas.

"The Cestrus River also flooded. Perhaps the gods are seeking to add your friend to the list of the dead."

"Our God is the Savior of men."

The doctor eyed Barnabas closely. "Your god is the God of the Jews?"

"Yes, we follow his Messiah. But how did you know?"

"The stripes. They are the thirty-nine, are they not? But he has been whipped more than once. Twice? He must be a rebellious one."

"You know much about the Jews."

"I am a God-fearer. I attend the synagogue occasionally."

Paul stirred. "A synagogue?"

The doctor stared at Paul in disbelief.

"Paul, in the name of sanity, go to sleep. Forget your call for a moment," begged Barnabas.

"What day is this?"

"Monday."

"I . . . we will be there."

"You can speak?"

"He is a Jew who wishes more than sanity or life to preach about his Lord to Gentiles like you."

"That's strange. Are you sure? Jews won't even talk to me."

"If someday you see us in the synagogue, please tell no one of my friend's illness."

"Oh, that," replied the doctor. "Disease is God's punishment? From the looks of his back, your God has punished him enough." The doctor turned and looked at Paul. Then he turned back to Barnabas. "I suspect that by next Sabbath your friend *will* be at the synagogue—or he will be dead. I lean to the latter."

"Be there. *I will be there*," struggled Paul.

The doctor shook his head and departed.

"You are insufferable, Paul of Tarsus," said Barnabas in dismay. "Now go to sleep."

"I'll be there."

"For your funeral! Go to sleep."

CHAPTER 12

For the next few days Paul did almost nothing but sleep. When he was awake, he drank great gulps of water but denied himself food. His fever raged for four days, finally breaking on Friday afternoon.

"I must go . . . tomorrow," he said. "Now, please go to the market and purchase some fruit." Barnabas protested the first request but was eager to do the second.

When Barnabas returned, he was chagrined to find Paul sitting up, his Pharisaic garb lying across his lap. Needle in hand, Paul was repairing the blue tassels that hung from the bottom of the robe.

"You may be as good with needle and cloth as you are with leather, but your hands are shaking wildly. You are too weak to be trying this. And you will *not* go to the synagogue tomorrow."

"Hand me your toga, Barnabas. Tomorrow you must look to be the best of Levites, and I the most healthy of Pharisees."

Barnabas laughingly threw up his hands and said, "Then may I, a Levite, point out to this devout Pharisee that it is already sundown? And you, my dear Pharisee, are sitting there working. You are desecrating the Sabbath."

"Jesus Christ nailed the Sabbath to the cross, my friend,"

retorted Paul smugly. "Along with several other things, I might add." Paul looked up from his work with a twinkle in his eye.

"Does Moses know this?" countered Barnabas.

"Yes, absolutely. Moses knows, but some of his followers don't."

"And how does Moses feel about this turn of events, the crucifixion of the Sabbath?" continued Barnabas, trying to laugh and talk at the same time.

"He is very glad. This Sabbath thing was a bit of a burden to him, you see. And frankly, I doubt he did a better job of observing it than you did!"

"If you live long enough—and I doubt you will—the Jews in this city will undoubtedly hear you tell them where the Sabbath ended up."

"Yes!" answered Paul. "Destroyed! Along with a few other things."

"All right, Paul, *what* other things?"

"Oh," sang Paul, not looking up as his needle shuttled in and out of Barnabas's Levitical garb, "such things as all six hundred laws of Moses . . . and . . ."

"Paul, I love you dearly, but you are half dead—and entirely mad. You are *far* too ill to go to the synagogue. But if you get there, and if you are allowed to speak, and if you say such things as this, be certain the other half of you will be dead before you leave."

"Ah, death—an excellent cure for madness," Paul responded, smiling broadly as he handed the mended clothes back to Barnabas. "But concerning Moses, the law, and all such things, you need not worry. I will not speak of these. No, if I am allowed to speak, it will be about Christ. Now, give me some fruit. And then I must sleep."

Barnabas sighed. "You would be there tomorrow if you knew it would be the last step before your grave, wouldn't you?"

"Yes, dear son of encouragement. And if you fail to wake me

at dawn tomorrow, you will henceforth be known as 'the son of Paul's temper.'"

The next morning Barnabas awoke at dawn, only to find Paul struggling futilely to rise from his bed. After several minutes of argument, Barnabas finally relented and handed Paul some fruit, then helped him to his feet.

A short time later he assisted Paul down the hall and into the daylight—the first natural light Paul had seen in a week. Paul pulled away from Barnabas.

"You'll never make it, Paul," Barnabas protested.

"Oh, you of little salt water!"

Slowly the two men made their way toward the city gate.

(Please keep in mind that several years later Paul and I entered this same town again. The inn, the synagogue, and the entire city of Antioch of Pisidia are very familiar to me.)

Should you ever visit Antioch of Pisidia, you will find it to be a city owned by Rome. It is walled and fortified. You enter through a large, unguarded gate. Almost immediately you will come to the center of the lower part of the city. The Forum of Tiberius is located on this lower level. Out from this spacious forum run many side streets, some as wide as five or even six feet. Crossing the forum, you can look up and see a second forum in the upper part of the city—the Forum of Augustus. (Incidentally, Antioch of Pisidia is the only city in the empire with *two* forums.)

You can reach the upper city by walking up a broad stairway with twelve steps. At the top of the steps you will pass through three arches. In this larger square, the Forum of Augustus, is a temple to their local god. His Latin name is *Men*—a god that is half man, half bull. One of the side streets branching off from the forum leads to a large open square. This is where the Jewish synagogue is located. Perhaps as many as fifty people gather in this synagogue on any given Sabbath.

The synagogue in Antioch of Pisidia is typical. Three-legged stools are scattered about, and benches are attached to the walls on three sides of the room. The doors to the synagogue are opened at about nine o'clock in the morning.

What happened on this particular Sabbath day, however, had never happened before in all history. It was an unprecedented hour. As I look back through all the years, I have to say that what happened that day in the provincial city of Antioch of Pisidia was a pivotal event in the history of the church. It was as important as Pentecost, and even as important as the day Peter preached in the home of Cornelius.

I have often heard my two friends retell what happened on that eventful day. Paul was weak with exhaustion, but he and Barnabas moved slowly toward the upper forum. Paul barely managed the twelve steps, but once they neared the synagogue, Paul drew on all his strength and walked into the synagogue almost athletically.

As in most cities in the empire, there are ten to fifteen thousand souls living in Antioch of Pisidia. Few visitors of note ever come to so isolated a place. This was even more true of the Jewish community. Rarely did a Jew from another city come through. Even news from Israel was rare. But on this day an unknown Pharisee, dressed in a white robe with blue tassels, marched boldly into the synagogue. (Paul could swagger with the best of the Pharisees if it served him!) Dressed in his traditional religious garb, he looked very imposing. One could feel the anticipation in the room as to what these visitors might share.

Paul and Barnabas seated themselves at the very back of the room, an excellent vantage point for searching out the God-fearers! Paul counted about twenty non-Jews, all seated in a separate section so they wouldn't contaminate the Jews.

Since his conversion, Paul had acquired a strong aversion to the Sabbath rituals of the synagogue. The service, with its readings from Moses and the Prophets, was devoid of participation by the people, and Paul found it to be a boring study in death and meaningless religion. The norm for Paul had become a living ecclesia, filled with chatting, excited participants. I often heard him say, "When God's people gather together, the meeting should not be dominated by any one person. The church belongs to all of the Lord's people." As to buildings and perfunctory ritual, Paul confessed that being in such places nearly made him ill. Whenever he had to endure such a traditional gathering, he would let his mind return to those wonderful, free-flowing Gentile meetings back in Syria.

As sick as Paul was that morning, his greater battle in that windowless room was simply to stay awake until the ritual ended. At last it did. Paul took a deep breath and steadied his body. By custom, he and Barnabas would be invited to speak. Sure enough, the manager of the synagogue looked over at the two strangers and said, "Brothers, if you have any word of encouragement for us, come and give it!" The intent of the invitation was, hopefully, to hear of any recent news from Jerusalem or other information of interest to a Jewish community.

Before Barnabas could blink, Paul rose to his feet. He started simply enough, but his voice rose as he delivered his stirring message. His listeners were enthralled, especially the God-fearing Gentiles, whom he specifically included.

Fortunately, Paul's words have been preserved for us. Just recently I was given a written account of this and other events as recorded by our dear brother Luke, the physician from Antioch of Syria. When I read Luke's account, I immediately recognized his source, for Paul had often told me of these same things. Lest you might be otherwise unaware of Luke's masterful account, I include his account of Paul's sermon in its entirety:

"People of Israel and you devout Gentiles who fear the God of Israel, listen to me.

"The God of this nation of Israel chose our ancestors and made them prosper in Egypt. Then he powerfully led them out of their slavery. He put up with them through forty years of wandering around in the wilderness. Then he destroyed seven nations in Canaan and gave their land to Israel as an inheritance. All this took about 450 years. After that, judges ruled until the time of Samuel the prophet. Then the people begged for a king, and God gave them Saul son of Kish, a man of the tribe of Benjamin, who reigned for forty years. But God removed him from the kingship and replaced him with David, a man about whom God said, 'David son of Jesse is a man after my own heart, for he will do everything I want him to.'

"And it is one of King David's descendants, Jesus, who is God's promised Savior of Israel! But before he came, John the Baptist preached the need for everyone in Israel to turn from sin and turn to God and be baptized. As John was finishing his ministry he asked, 'Do you think I am the Messiah? No! But he is coming soon—and I am not even worthy to be his slave.'"

The people of Antioch of Pisidia had never heard of John the Baptist, but when Paul announced that the Messiah had already come and that his name was Jesus, a shock ran through the synagogue! Jews and God-fearing Gentiles alike leaned forward to hear every word from this visiting Pharisee.

"Brothers—you sons of Abraham, and also all of you devout Gentiles who fear the God of Israel—this salvation is for us! The people in Jerusalem and their leaders fulfilled prophecy by condemning Jesus to death. They didn't recognize him or realize that he is the one the prophets had written about, though they hear the prophets' words read every Sabbath.

They found no just cause to execute him, but they asked Pilate to have him killed anyway.

"When they had fulfilled all the prophecies concerning his death, they took him down from the cross and placed him in a tomb. But God raised him from the dead! And he appeared over a period of many days to those who had gone with him from Galilee to Jerusalem—these are his witnesses to the people of Israel."

A second shock ran through the room when Paul mentioned the Crucifixion. All present had witnessed that gruesome style of Roman execution. Probably some of the Jews had heard of Jesus' crucifixion. The Gentiles, on the other hand, had never heard of Jesus, but they listened intently to Paul's every word. As he spoke, his eyes boring into his audience, it all sounded astoundingly real.

When Paul said that Jesus had been raised from the dead after having been crucified, people began whispering to one another. They had never heard such things before, and they had certainly not expected to hear such news when they came to their regular Sabbath service! Paul continued:

"And now Barnabas and I are here to bring you this Good News. God's promise to our ancestors has come true in our own time, in that God raised Jesus. This is what the second psalm is talking about when it says concerning Jesus, 'You are my Son. Today I have become your Father.' For God had promised to raise him from the dead, never again to die. This is stated in the Scripture that says, 'I will give you the sacred blessings I promised to David.' Another psalm explains more fully, saying, 'You will not allow your Holy One to rot in the grave.' Now this is not a reference to David, for after David had served his generation according to the will of God, he died and was buried, and his body decayed. No, it was a reference to someone else—someone whom God raised and whose body did not decay."

The devout people in the synagogue were intimately familiar with the passages of Scripture Paul was quoting, but they had never heard them applied to the Messiah. And they had certainly not been taught that these prophecies had already been fulfilled! A buzz began to run through the room, causing Paul to lift his hand to quiet them.

"Brothers, listen! In this man Jesus there is forgiveness for your sins. Everyone who believes in him is freed from all guilt and declared right with God—something the Jewish law could never do. Be careful! Don't let the prophets' words apply to you. For they said,

'Look, you mockers,
be amazed and die!
For I am doing something in your own day,
something you wouldn't believe
even if someone told you about it.'"

What Paul did that morning was, in some ways, a tribute to Stephen. Much of Paul's message was a retelling of the message he had heard years earlier on the day Stephen was killed. It was as though Paul was repaying a debt to a man whose influence on his own conversion had been so great. Paul knew Stephen's words were powerful because of what those very words had done to him.

But just as Stephen's message had brought down the wrath of the Jewish leaders, Paul angered the leaders of the synagogue when he implied that the words of Habakkuk applied to them— that they were mockers worthy of death! Further, they were galled when he said the Jewish law had never been able to provide that freedom from guilt.

Freedom! Most of the Gentiles in that room were slaves.

To them, Paul's words were unbelievable, yet wonderful. And his message that the Messiah had come was even more wonderful.

When the synagogue leaders dismissed the meeting, Paul and Barnabas moved toward the door. As they did, the Gentiles came rushing up to them, asking questions and following the two men into the courtyard. "Come back next Sabbath; tell us more," they pleaded.

Paul was both surprised and elated, yet it was exactly what he had hoped would happen. Slowly he and Barnabas made their way out into the Forum of Augustus, with most of the Gentiles still following. It was as though they had already become believers. It was a remarkable morning. As Paul and Barnabas moved toward the inn, Paul called out to the Gentiles he had seen in the synagogue, "By God's grace, remain faithful!"

∞

Paul managed somehow to get back to his room, where he collapsed on the pallet of straw. The fever returned immediately and continued for the next three days. But Barnabas had no doubt that Paul would be stronger by the next Sabbath. Nothing encouraged our brother Paul like seeing Gentiles becoming interested in Jesus Christ.

No one saw Paul during that week. Barnabas was seen only a few times in the market, as he was busy caring for Paul. But the rumor of their presence and what they said to the people in the synagogue was spreading everywhere.

A Messiah. A death by crucifixion. A man rising out of his own grave. Freedom! Freedom from guilt. Freedom from *everything*. It was the news of the year. Everyone wanted to hear these men's wild claims. An entire Gentile city in the far reaches of Galatia was talking about a Jew named Jesus.

Paul was euphoric. By dawn of the next Sabbath, people of the city had begun filling the small square outside the synagogue. By nine o'clock the street was backed up, and people were spilling into the Forum of Augustus, hoping to see and hear these men.

"Never," exclaimed Paul. "I never expected to see anything like this." He and Barnabas worked their way through the crowd and finally to the door of the synagogue. But the door was *locked*.

"No surprise here," said Barnabas.

"If they won't let us into the synagogue, we will speak to the people here in the square," said Paul as he turned to face the throng.

But before he could begin speaking, the synagogue doors swung open. The manager of the synagogue came out and immediately began yelling to the people, "These men lie. They are dishonest. The story they tell is not true. Do not listen to them." Others came out. One of them swore a curse upon Paul. Another upon Barnabas.

Paul began addressing the crowd, but one of the synagogue leaders shoved him aside. A hush settled across the square as the people watched. Then Paul turned and spoke to the men in the doorway of the synagogue, but he spoke so loudly that his voice carried across the crowded square. Thousands of Gentile ears heard his every word.

"It was necessary that this Good News from God be given first to you Jews. But since you have rejected it and judged yourselves unworthy of eternal life—"

The crowd roared with laughter. The Jewish officials were beside themselves with anger. Paul quieted the crowd and continued. "Since you have rejected it and judged yourselves unworthy of eternal life—well, we will offer it to the Gentiles. For this is as the Lord commanded us when he said, 'I have made you a light to the Gentiles, to bring salvation to the farthest corners of the earth.'"

When Paul mentioned the Gentiles, the synagogue leader

clenched his fist and shook it at Paul. The crowd roared its approval. Paul continued, speaking directly to the men in the doorway. "Let it never be forgotten that the news of Jesus Christ came to you *first*. For it is the will of God that the Hebrews always be first. But this day you have rejected your own Lord."

Paul paused, his eyes flashing. "Now look at us. From this moment forward, we will declare God's message of salvation and freedom to the Gentiles—to the uncircumcised, unclean *heathen!*" The crowd erupted, hooting and applauding and cheering. And at that moment, those heathen who were appointed to eternal life believed Paul's message.

Paul cried out to the crowd, "Follow me to the forum." Everyone rushed eagerly to the Forum of Augustus. Paul leaped up onto the pedestal of the statue of Men in front of the temple.

"We will meet again tomorrow just after dawn. Then we will share with you more about your Lord. But we need a place to gather. Who has a room to lend us?"

"I do!" exclaimed a man who was at that very moment becoming a new believer in Christ. "Down that street, the last door."

Everyone looked in the direction the man pointed. "Your name, sir?" asked Barnabas.

"I am the son of Jupiter."

Paul could not help but laugh. He enjoyed the irony. The first person in the city to openly respond to the gospel of Jesus was a man who carried the name of the preeminent heathen god. Paul was elated. "All right, son of Jupiter," cried Paul gleefully, "may we meet in your home just after dawn tomorrow morning?"

"You may."

"But, sir," came a voice. "Can we meet earlier? I am a slave. My duties to my master begin before dawn and last until nightfall."

Others in the crowd nodded in agreement. Paul grasped the dilemma and made the most of it. "Could you come after dark?" he asked, recognizing that over half the people in the city were slaves.

"That is a great problem, sir, for the streets are too dangerous after dark," came an anxious voice.

For a brief instant Paul and Barnabas were at a loss as to how to respond to this problem. But a solution was proposed by a booming voice from the crowd. "Wait!" A man stepped boldly up onto the pedestal beside Paul and whispered to him. Paul grinned, then raised his hand. He motioned to the man to speak. "Tomorrow night the streets of Antioch will be safe. I am head of the garrison of soldiers stationed here, and I will place a guard at the gate at dusk. There will also be a guard in both the Forum of Tiberius and here in the Forum of Augustus. Both courtyards will also be lit by lamps and torches. At the front of the street that leads to the house of Jupiter's son, there will be another guard. Another will be at his door. I, too, will be present. I am Dardanus, of the Roman Legion. By the gods, you *will* be safe."

Paul was astounded. Soldiers of Rome, who never guarded anyone except the elite of the city and who saw justice as being only for the rich and the soldiers, now proposed to protect *slaves.* "Son of Jupiter," said Paul, addressing his new host, "dare we ask if your hospitality could be extended to us both morning and night?"

"My heart leaps, sir, until it inhabits my breast no more. My house is yours."

"So be it," thundered Barnabas as he watched the light of Christ break forth on face after face. Paul, Barnabas, and Dardanus stepped down from the base of the statue.

At that moment an old man pushed his way through the crowd until he came to Paul. He was crying. Paul recognized the old man, for he had been in the synagogue the week before.

"Your God," the man said through his tears. "He rose? He lives?"

"Yes."

"Did you see him rise?" The old man's eyes moved back and forth to examine the faces of both Paul and Barnabas. Paul stiffened. This was a moment when John Mark should have been present, for Mark had seen the resurrected Lord.

"My nephew saw him die and stood face-to-face with him after he came back to life," replied Barnabas.

"I, too, have seen him face-to-face," added Paul.

The old man grasped Paul's garment. "I will die soon. You have seen him? Is this the truth?"

"I spoke to him. In terror, but I spoke to him. I had persecuted him; I would not believe; my heart was closed to him. But he came to me from heaven, and as I stood in his presence, he struck me blind!"

The old man moved his hands before Paul's eyes. "How long blind?"

"Three days."

"And . . . ?"

"I believed!"

"And . . . ?"

"He is in me."

"In you! Where?"

"Here!" Paul struck his breast.

The old man stared at Paul, then Barnabas, then struck his own breast. "I think . . . here . . . also!" he replied, his ancient eyes a wellspring of tears. "I will see you at night and at morning. I have served my master fifty-five years. I am a Phrygian, a slave. Now that I am old my master lets me sleep until the sun clears the horizon, and my duties end when the sun touches the earth again."

Paul took the old man's hands and ran his fingers across the scars on the old man's wrists. "A Phrygian."

"Most of the slaves here are of my race. Almost all."

"Brother, you are a slave no longer. This day you have been set free by the one who now lives inside you."

"Yes," wept the old man. "I know."

The three men embraced and together cried. To their surprise, several others standing near them came and joined the embrace and the tears.

A few moments later Barnabas had to grab Paul, who had almost fainted. "Help me, Barnabas," he whispered.

"All right, but they will see that you are sick."

"Who cares?" Paul whispered back with a smile. "The heathen don't know that God punishes men like me for being so sinful."

"And we won't tell them," laughed Barnabas.

The two men pushed their way through the crowd back toward the city gate. Friendly hands reached out to touch them as they passed. "We'll see you before dawn tomorrow—at the home of the son of Jupiter," Barnabas called out. "Pass the word to your friends."

"If I live a hundred years, I will never see a grander hour than this," said Paul as they passed through the city gates.

"Nor I. And I saw Pentecost. But you, my friend, don't need to worry about living a hundred years. You won't. I'm not at all sure you'll live till dawn!"

"Well, if I don't, *you* be there tomorrow! In the home of that son of Jupiter. And tell him he is now the son of the ever living God!"

The two men laughed and cried and then broke into thanksgiving to God.

"He did it all. God did it all," Paul said later as he fell asleep. Barnabas sat down next to his sleeping friend, a smile on his face and tears in his eyes. But little could either of them have guessed what lay ahead.

CHAPTER 13

When Paul and Barnabas reached the house of the son of Jupiter the next morning, they found a large room already full of eager Gentiles. Many had to stand.

Paul was too ill to speak, so that joy fell to Barnabas. The first thing he did was teach everyone how to sing a psalm. They loved it.

Then, sitting on the floor, Barnabas told his story. Most of these Gentiles had never been to the synagogue, so they had no context for knowing how to conduct themselves. Over and again they interrupted Barnabas with questions and comments. Barnabas loved it. His wit brought smiles and laughter to a roomful of people who rarely smiled, more rarely laughed, and had never sung. When Barnabas was finally able to bring his message to a conclusion, they sang again. And again. Paul wept through the entire meeting.

The meeting ended, or so it seemed, but no one departed. Everyone wanted to stay with the others just a little longer. On and on they talked. The primary subjects of discussion were how often they could meet and how they would get to all the gatherings. For a room filled mostly with slaves, there was no lack of variety. Discussion was fervent. Finally, they turned to

Barnabas and asked, "Can you come every morning and every evening? There will always be someone here."

Barnabas and Paul looked at each other in wonder. Paul asked, *"Every* morning, *every* night?"

"Yes," they responded. "That way everyone will have a chance to participate in the meetings."

"All right," Paul agreed. "And I'll feel stronger later, and then I'll tell you *my* story."

Paul and Barnabas could not have guessed they would be telling their stories and the stories of others over and over to a people who never tired of hearing them—or of interrupting! Finally, reluctantly, an impoverished people now brimming with the life of God left the meeting place as ones set free—back to their slavery, yet not slaves at all.

Paul slept the entire day. That night there were again torches and guards, just as Dardanus had promised. And, as promised, Paul told his story. But not before these new holy ones had sung the psalm Barnabas taught them, over and over again.

This was not a synagogue! These new believers got up and walked around, talked to one another even as Paul talked, and interrupted Paul continually. Once Dardanus got up, walked to the door, and yelled orders at the guards. Everyone laughed, and Paul could not have been more pleased. He had at last found his true home.

That night these *almost* heathen, not-fully-Christian Gentiles learned another song. There was no counting how many times those dear people sang those two songs. By the time I met them, several years later, they were singing like the angels at Bethlehem, and they seemed to know a thousand songs by heart.

As the days unfolded, the new believers became ingenious at ways of helping one another get to the meetings. They exchanged tasks, took one another's place, and escorted one another through the city in groups. One thing dominated their lives above all else: They loved being together. Each morning and each evening they stayed longer and talked more. Little by little you could see their conversations turn more to Christ.

Paul continued his slow recovery. In the meantime, new things began to take place in the lives of these Gentiles. Amazing things.

Paul and Barnabas moved to an inn inside the city walls. One day when Paul returned to his room, he found a meal prepared for him, laid out beautifully on the floor. "The sisters," he whispered. "God bless them." It was all he could say, for he knew their poverty, and this meal was no small thing. This meal, this gesture of love, was something these people had never known before. Poverty was too great, life too hard for such things as kindness and giving. Further, these dear ones had *nothing* to give. Paul stared at the meal spread out in his room, knowing the enormous sacrifice it represented. If there were 15,000 people in Antioch of Pisidia, perhaps 500 of them—a handful of wealthy Greek and Jewish merchants—used money. The other 14,500 traded and bartered. For them a handful of grain constituted a day's earning, and that was barely enough to feed a family. *This* meal represented a truly sacrificial gift from perhaps a dozen households. Each sister had taken a little food from her family's daily portion of grain, and out of newborn love for Christ and for one another, they had created this meal!

Paul bowed before the meal and wept. Then he relished it for more than an hour as he thanked God and wept over every bite. The love of Christ in these new believers was finding divine expression from within. As Paul ate, he repeated the name of every believer in the ecclesia.

This deep, indescribable love for one another is known only by the people of God who are in the community of the ecclesia. I have seen it nowhere else.

In a city such as Antioch of Pisidia, where most are slaves, those who are free are often worse off than slaves, for the slaves at least know they will have food to eat. The freed men—slaves who have been set free—must go to the market every day at dawn in hopes of finding someone who needs their backs and hands. When they are hired, which is rare, they are given a choice of payment: one denarius or a single-hand scoop of grain. In winter, on days of rain, and on many other days, freed men find no work at all.

During the course of a year, some who have rooms lose them because they have no money or nothing left with which to barter. During the winter, some barter all they own for food. In this region of Galatia, many slaves, when given the opportunity, refuse to be set free. Others, once freed and on the edge of starvation, sell themselves back into slavery. Hardship is a constant companion in the lives of these people. Such are the people who make up the community of believers in Pisidia.

A group of people have become brothers and sisters, their new way of life wonderful and joyful. It is a way of living never before seen on the face of the earth. Yet God ordained that it come into being in this poor and remote region of Asia Minor.

It is amazing, as I look back, to see how these holy ones take care of one another. If one brother finds a job in the marketplace and the supervisor needs more help, that brother runs to find another brother so he, too, can work that day.

When several brothers work together, they work harder and better. They share a spirit of joy, often singing, often praising. Though the masters and supervisors don't understand it, they remember these men who work so well together. As they hire workers each morning in the marketplace, they search out these faces first. Some of the merchants have been known to say: "You, today you work. Go find your friends, the ones you call *brothers*, the ones you laugh and sing with."

In the gatherings, brothers tell one another about possible

places to look for a day's work. The next night they tell *everyone* about how the Lord provided them a job, while the rest listen, rejoice, laugh, and interrupt.

Nor were the brothers alone in this new way of meeting needs. This new life inside them was changing everyone and everything, affecting the women as much as the men. The sisters in Pisidia began caring for one another, a phenomenon unknown in the Gentile world. They care for one another in the most unexpected ways. In childbirth, of course, but also working together at the river and in their homes and rooms. (Those who have no home and have to sleep in the forum are *especially* cared for.) Any sister who becomes sick is soon cared for throughout the night and day.

I have often seen the sisters working together in the fields, caring for one another's children, sharing vegetables and grain with one another, or cleaning rooms together. Sometimes they meet only to sing, to talk, to cry, to care, and to be cared for. If one somehow manages to have more than a day's supply of food, they often come together and prepare one big meal so all can have a good meal that day.

All of this happened without Paul or Barnabas ever telling them that *this* is what believers in ecclesia just naturally do together.

Amazingly, all that I relate to you here emerged spontaneously within only a few weeks after their redemption in Christ. In the brief *four months* that Paul and Barnabas were in Antioch of Pisidia, this wonderful new way of life had become a natural part of all their lives.

One incident that took place during those early days was told to me again and again and always with laughter and joy. It involved a brother named Epitheus, who was a Phrygian slave. Epitheus had a hard master. One day he did something that displeased his master, and at the close of the day he was terribly beaten. That night, bloody and scared, Epitheus slipped quietly into the meeting. Everyone recognized that he had been beaten, but they insisted Epitheus tell what had happened. Epitheus was reluctant, for he was despondent and in much pain.

Paul began talking to Epitheus. The room fell silent. I do not know exactly what Paul said, except that he began to tell Epitheus about the high place that he, Epitheus, held in Christ. As Paul continued, everyone in the room began to cheer and cry. Then Barnabas trumpeted an exhortation to Epitheus that shook the room. (A Roman guard came running to the place of the meeting thinking it was a riot. He looked in and muttered, "Oh, it's only them.") All the holy ones came to their feet and pressed in around Epitheus, calling out exhortations and encouragement and telling him what he looked like to God through Christ. But the high moment came when Epitheus began to exhort the others and to claim that high place in Christ. Suddenly Epitheus looked like a king, and his master a slave. Everyone was shouting, praising, and crying. It was a most glorious hour, ending just before dawn in hugs and embraces.

Then there was the crisis that arose when Dardanus was ordered to war.

CHAPTER 14

Dardanus was ordered out of Pisidia to join a Roman army marching to the border of the Germanic tribes. This left the brothers and sisters with no way to go to and return from the morning and evening gatherings.

This did not stop the brothers' ingenuity, however. When a meeting ended, all the holy ones departed together, first seeing the sisters safely home, then escorting those who lived the farthest away. Gradually the group worked its way back toward the center of the city until a remaining few came back to brother Jupiter's house. The last two or three brothers who lived nearby then went to their apartments. If this did not work out, the last few men spent the night in Jupiter's living room. I know of no brother or sister who has ever been robbed or hurt in Antioch of Pisidia. (Even to this day it is the holy ones and no others who dare to travel the streets of that town at night.)

The whole city, of course, was soon speaking of all these odd things. Nor was that the only thing that caught the city's attention. One day several brothers met in the marketplace by accident. They were soon laughing and praising their Lord. Then one began to sing. All joined in, for the Holy Spirit was overflowing in all of them. In a few moments, other believers who heard the singing came running to the square and joined in. The city had never seen such a thing. Singing? For men to *smile* was rare. That they *laughed* was unprecedented. That they *sang*, unbelievable!

There were Greek and Jewish merchants from other towns who were in the square that day. They inquired as to who these people were and why they were so joyful. From this, and from other stories told in the city, people in towns and villages as far as fifty miles away began to hear about Jesus and his smiling followers.

In the meantime Paul had fully recovered, and he began going to the marketplace to look for work. In the beginning very few asked for his skills. There was, in fact, no way for Paul to earn grain or enough denarii to live on. Every day the wealthy sent some of their skilled slaves to the marketplace with instructions to underbid any free man who had the same skills. The slave always got the work and returned to his master in the evening with either grain or a denarius. As a result, Paul, like any other free man, was almost always underbid. But Paul did begin to find work—because of the brothers in the ecclesia. Slaves who came to Jupiter's living room began telling their masters about Paul and how trustworthy and skilled he was. "He is an honest man, a good man, highly skilled, who works fast and is as good or better than any man with such a skill." To Romans they added, "And he is a citizen of the city of Rome."

It was not long before work was coming to Paul from both the marketplace and the villas outside the city. It seemed that certain slaves were pointing out to their masters that there were leather goods needing to be made or repaired, or that a new tent or canopy was sorely needed.

Paul even took on an apprentice—named *Barnabas!* And a quick learner Barnabas turned out to be. Before they were beaten and thrown from the city, Antioch of Pisidia had two very good workers making and repairing tents, awnings, harnesses, sandals, and other goods of leather, cotton, canvas, and goat hair.

Often a brother or sister would come by to talk with the two men as they carried on their work. Rarely did Paul or Barnabas find it necessary to draw water for themselves. Someone was always there to bring them something to drink. As darkness came, when merchants and workers folded their shops, there was usually someone ready to help the two men roll up their canvas and carry their things back to their room.

One day a brother named Timenius sat down in front of Barnabas and asked, "Would you tell me of Stephen's death?" Barnabas readily agreed to tell the story.

"Now tell me of your first visit to Antioch of Syria and going to find Paul in Tarsus," the brother said. Again Barnabas complied with the request, not inquiring as to the reason for this strange request.

To Barnabas's delight, Timenius then repeated the entire story back to Barnabas. Barnabas, in turn, corrected any errors in the story. By evening Timenius could retell the story back to Barnabas word for word.

In general, the people living in Antioch of Pisidia (and this is true throughout Galatia) are illiterate, but that does not mean they are ignorant. Timenius was a bridge builder and architect. He could speak for hours on end regarding the details and intricacies of building roads, bridges, and government buildings. He was a living book on this subject. No one knew architecture better. He taught those who worked with him, repeating the knowledge and instruction he had learned as a youth, plus all he had learned over a lifetime. He had a remarkable mind. Yet Timenius was a slave. He had never once held a coin of his own in his hand nor slept in a room with fewer than ten people in it.

A real surprise awaited Barnabas at the end of the next day. Timenius asked permission to repeat the story once more.

Barnabas nodded, but he and Paul were startled when Timenius began. He was telling the story not in Greek or Latin but in his own native dialect, and that with great flourish.

The two men laughed, then applauded, as they realized what Timenius had done. Though he had spent the day listening to Barnabas tell the gospel stories in Greek, he would now retell the stories to his slave friends who knew only the Phrygian dialect. "I will return next week, with my master's permission," he said, "so that you can tell me more of the wonderful news of Jesus."

Others came to the marketplace for the same reason. This is the primary means of learning among those who are unschooled. Barnabas was their favorite repeater, for it took a unique person to follow Paul's wordings, and repeating what he said was more difficult. But Paul adapted. Sometimes he was very good at turning the mysteries of God into simple stories. (We have Barnabas to thank for that, for Paul learned this from Barnabas's example.)

Sisters also came, bringing a few small millet cakes, then asking questions, telling stories of their people, and learning to sing psalms from the two makers of tents. They, too, sat and repeated stories back to Barnabas until they could tell them as well as, or *better* than, he did!

I have listened to the holy ones in Pisidia tell me all about that first visit of Paul and Barnabas to their region. I have also heard them tell, in painful detail, how the two men were beaten and thrown out of the city, for it was a very dramatic experience for them all.

CHAPTER 15

The two church planters were in Antioch of Pisidia for four months. That is not long. Remember, most of the holy ones in the ecclesia were slaves. There were one or two Greeks and Jews and a few soldiers. There were no city leaders or persons of influence.

All the God-fearers who heard Paul that first day were now strong believers, and they no longer attended the synagogue. Having been part of the body of Christ and tasted his freedom, and having become one with others in the gathering, they could not stand the thought of going back to the synagogue.

By the time the two apostles left Pisidia, there were about one hundred adults in the ecclesia. (To the rest of the city they probably seemed like thousands because of their exuberance and their unique way of life.) Of that hundred, only six men could read. And only one of the six could write. Remember this as you consider how brief a time these two men were in Pisidia to help the ecclesia there. These new believers had no building, no ritual, no priestlike leaders. No leaders at all, in fact. This was the only religion whose adherents met in homes. And those dear believers had no holy writings—Jewish or Christian—when the two apostles left.

What ended Paul and Barnabas's presence in Pisidia?

Jacob, the ruler of the synagogue, despised Paul. He ranted against him constantly. This was of little concern to anyone until one morning when three unbelieving Hebrews crept into an early-morning gathering. They came, watched, and then believed! They had never seen anything like this group that evidenced such joy—singing, sharing, interrupting, hugging, loving, and then more sharing. All of this centered around Jesus Christ, each person telling how they had experienced him that day. All this won the hearts of the three Hebrews.

When Jacob heard of the conversion of these Jews, he was outraged. He knew exactly what he would do to stop these people. He would turn the local Romans against them! Roman protection, Roman justice, Roman fairness was only for Romans, their soldiers, the wealthy, and the local leaders whom they appointed. Slaves and freed men were never included in Roman justice, nor were the city leaders concerned about extending justice or protection to such people.

Jacob dared not take his contention directly to the Roman rulers, however. He didn't even go directly to the leaders of the city. He went to their wives, who were influential in the cult of the god Men. Using his position as a religious leader in the community, Jacob went to the leading women and began telling them of the danger Paul posed to the city. He presented Paul's teachings as undermining the authority of the local god (which was true), but he also twisted Paul's words to make them sound dangerous to the stability and welfare of the larger community. The women were alarmed on both counts. They didn't want their own influence as religious leaders reduced, and they were fearful about what the Roman rulers might do if the leadership of the community was undermined. These women, therefore, took Jacob's deceiving words to their husbands. Problems in local government make Roman rulers unhappy. This problem would be dealt with swiftly.

While Barnabas sat working in the marketplace one day,

guards came, seized him, and dragged him before the city fathers. Other soldiers searched the marketplace for Paul. The city officials had already gathered in the square in front of the governing hall, awaiting the arrival of the two troublemakers. Barnabas knew the gravity of the situation as soon as he arrived in the square. He had heard that some of the influential women were complaining about the new religion, but he was surprised to see the city's magistrate sitting in council.

Even more disturbing was the sight of two lictors standing on either side of the magistrate. Lictors, representing the power of Rome, were men who beat people with rods. At their feet lay the *fasces*, an ancient symbol of Roman authority. It was a bundle of wooden rods bound tightly around the handle of an ax, leaving the axhead extending out between the rods. The local government was not going to risk a religious disturbance in their city, so they had enlisted the assistance of the Roman rulers. It was a foregone conclusion that Paul and Barnabas would be beaten.

The proceedings began, and the entire square was full of eager onlookers.

"I was told there were two of them," said the magistrate. "Where is the other one?"

"He is still being sought."

"You. What is your name?"

"Barnabas."

"A Jew?"

"I am."

"You are teaching a new and foreign religion. That is prohibited."

"But . . ."

"You will leave this city immediately. You will take your god with you. You are banished from this city forever. Never return."

"But . . ."

The magistrate nodded to the lictors. They reached down and began unbinding the fasces, each searching for the strongest of the rods. A soldier grabbed Barnabas's arms and pulled him over a waist-high whipping pillar. It was stained with the blood of past victims of such beatings.

At that moment a squad of soldiers found Paul, who had been trimming sheepskin in another area of the market. The soldiers grabbed Paul and half dragged him to the square. Paul caught sight of Barnabas just as the lictors prepared to beat him. He reached up to the *diptych* hanging around his neck and pushed it down into his toga. That diptych could have spared Paul, a citizen of Rome, such a beating; but Paul was not going to stand behind his rights to be spared a beating already being administered to Barnabas.

One lictor had taken his place on one side of Barnabas, the other lictor on the other side. Together they ripped off Barnabas's shirt. One lictor raised his rod above his head and brought it down hard on Barnabas's back. The crowd squealed with delight. The other lictor followed with an equally hard stroke. The lictors quickly established a rhythm to striking their victim. The rods were whistling through the air with each blow. Barnabas's back was soon red from waist to neck. Just before the rods broke his skin, the beating ended, the soldiers released his arms, and Barnabas crumbled to the pavement, almost unconscious.

"We have the other one."

"Good. Continue."

Paul was dragged forward and pulled over the same marble column.

"On what charge?" Paul asked loudly.

"Your companion will tell you when he finds his tongue," barked the magistrate. The crowd roared with laughter.

One lictor tore off Paul's shirt. There was a moment of silence as the lictor and the crowd caught sight of Paul's gnarled back. The magistrate leaned forward. A sound of delight rose from the crowd. "The Jews don't like you either, do they?" said the magistrate.

With fiendish glee in their eyes, the lictors reached for their rods, determined to give Paul a beating no Jewish whip could match. The first lictor slammed his rod down on Paul's back with all his might. The second lictor hit him with a vengeance. Nor did they stop when his back turned red. Soon a mist of Paul's blood filled the air and splattered on the lictors' faces. They stopped only when Paul slumped forward unconscious.

Years later Paul told me that he almost cried out, *"Civis Romanus sum,"* just before he fainted.

Three times I was beaten with rods.

Paul's body crumpled to the pavement. "Get him out of here," ordered the magistrate. The soldiers nodded. But just before they dragged him away, one of the brothers, himself a soldier, stepped forward and did a most courageous thing. Forcing his way past the other soldiers, he knelt down and picked Paul up in his arms, glared defiantly at the soldiers, the magistrate, and the crowd, and then carried Paul to Jupiter's home. A few minutes later Barnabas staggered into the same house.

Late that night something incredible began to unfold.

CHAPTER 16

It was midnight. The house was packed. This would be the last opportunity for the believers to meet together with Paul and Barnabas. Virtually every believer in Antioch of Pisidia had managed to find a way to be in Jupiter's home that evening.

Although most had to stand for hours, they listened as Barnabas presented all kinds of practical advice. Questions flowed from the brothers and sisters. This was, after all, a farewell to a fragile young ecclesia that had been planted in a hostile city only four months before. Every minute counted. Every question was important, and every answer held sacred. Yet it was obvious that these dear people believed they would survive and even flourish. There was even anticipation in the air.

Paul came into the room later, still in great pain. As he spoke, he added spiritual instructions, lacing them with practical help. Little by little the two men managed to give instruction and encouragement that would remain after they were gone. That night a coherent means for surviving the future began to emerge before the Lord's people.

Barnabas ended the night with an exhortation. "Before most of you were baptized, I told you that following the Lord Jesus Christ would bring you to an hour such as this. And so it has come. You are social outcasts in your own city. People stare at you in the market; they sneer and speak evil of you. If they have not done so already, they will. Rumors—outrageous rumors—will fill this city concerning you. For some of you, your masters will have grave questions about what you are doing when you are with the other believers. Others of you will find it more difficult than before to be hired in the marketplace. Sisters, you will feel the sting of rejection when you are in the city or at the river. Stay together as much as possible. Draw your strength from the Lord and from one another.

"Brothers, it is your responsibility—no one man or group of men, but all of you—to direct and lead the church. Look to Christ, who is your only head. He is alive. He is *in* you. He can lead his body. We are leaving you with no appointed leaders. But you have much experience at being together and working together. You already knew that one day you would be left alone, for we have warned you often. We have prepared you for this hour.

"Finally, remember that I often told you of the slander, the whip, and the rod experienced in Jerusalem, but remember also the *joy* your fellow believers in Judea experienced when they went through similar ordeals. Even as I told you their stories, you wondered if you might one day be counted worthy of such suffering and such joy for Christ's sake. That hour has come. Now Paul and I must bid you good-bye. Under orders of the authorities, we must leave this city.

"The Lord Jesus *has* counted you worthy, and he is dwelling in each of you. He is the head of the church. He is triumphant, and his body is triumphant. The sun will soon rise. A good foundation has been laid here: His name is Jesus Christ. Brothers and sisters, you can make it. You need no more outside help, and you need no leaders within."

With joy the brothers and sisters heard these things. Years later they told me of that night. It was with a sense of pride that they recounted Barnabas's words and how *all* of this came to be true.

When Barnabas had finished his exhortation, all the holy ones knelt together around him and Paul and began to offer quiet prayers. The prayers turned into whispered songs. Then everyone moved into the streets.

Outside two soldiers, both believers, were waiting. One of them spoke in mock sternness. "Enemy of Rome, it is my duty to escort you to the border of this province."

Paul smiled. "It is a good escort." The two brothers returned his smile.

That night every member of the body of Christ in Antioch slipped through the gates and out onto the road. Immediately a song exploded. They began to laugh at their own boldness. Cheers rose. Shouts followed. Exhortations, loud and fervent, filled the darkness. For nearly an hour the songs rose, calling forth the morning's light. Then came embraces, tears, and more exhortations. Paul brought the last word. It was like a thunderclap filled with joy and hope.

"We leave you to Christ alone. We leave you, the body, to your Lord, the head. You have no school as the heathen do. You have no buildings as the Hebrews do. You have no books as the learned do." Paul paused. His eyes twinkled. "And little good such books would do you, since most of you can't read!" Everyone laughed, then cheered.

"Unlike other religions, we leave you with no leaders, no priests. We leave you with no scrolls. And don't bother to think the synagogue will let you use theirs!" Everyone roared with laughter. "We leave you to brotherhood and sisterhood, to the unity and oneness that you already know so well, and to the awesomeness of being the body of Christ. We leave you to the guardianship of your love for one another. We leave you to the front room of Jupiter's house."

The son of Jupiter shouted a welcome to everyone. "You

can meet there and also *live* there if need be." This, too, was met with a roar of approval.

"But most of all," Paul continued, "we leave you to an indwelling Lord, one whom you know and daily experience. We leave you to Christ alone!"

To the delight of all, Paul then reached down and took off his sandals. Holding both sandals in his hands, he began shaking them furiously. (Everyone remembered what the two men had told them about the words of Jesus.) They began to applaud. Barnabas pounded his sandals on the Roman mileage marker beside the road. The scene was one of joy; the holy ones were euphoric.

What followed cannot be described. If you have experienced such a moment, you need no explanation, and if you have not, no description would be adequate. Suffice it to say that the two men who planted the assembly in Antioch of Pisidia departed that night amid unbelievable rejoicing. As Paul and Barnabas walked down the Augustan Road, the holy ones returned to the city to carry on as the living expression of Christ on this earth. They were leaderless and alone, and they were hundreds of miles from any other believers; in fact, they had never laid eyes on any other assembly, nor any other followers of Christ.

But the adventure had only begun.

CHAPTER 17

Paul, this road leads back toward our home in Syria. Your body cannot take much more of this. We planted an assembly in the midst of a heathen nation. What do you think? Dare we enter another city, or should we go home?"

For a moment Paul was silent. "Only *one* Gentile church. Just *one*. Shall the gospel of Christ and his ecclesia be found in only one city? Among all the Gentiles of this world, one ecclesia? There are seventy-five million souls in the empire, and only one Gentile witness of believers who gather together in his name. Among all the uncircumcised, shall there be only *one* witness?

"In Judah and Galilee there are fewer than a million souls, yet several hundred towns and villages already have assemblies of believers. Besides that, there are twelve men in Israel to plant more churches. Twelve men for a million people. We are *two!* In all the heathen nations, only two men have been sent out to plant Gentile churches. Two church planters for *seventy-five million* souls. And all we have done is plant *one* ecclesia, and that one is in an obscure city in a little-known province. Do not the heathen nations deserve better?"

"But it is a beautiful expression of Christ's bride, Paul—as beautiful as any on earth."

"Yes. Perhaps the most beautiful of all. So let there be more of them!"

"Paul, it is true that we are only two, but *one* of us is very beaten up."

Barnabas's words reminded Paul of the searing pain in his back. He stifled a cough. "All right, let us take the Augustan Road. Shall we go to the right or the left?"

"If we turn to the right, it will lead us back home."

"Barnabas," asked Paul, speaking pensively, "which is the safer route to Antioch of Syria—by ship or by road?"

"Are you serious? By this road."

"Then let us return home, as you suggest. But we can travel east as well as south. There are many cities, Gentile cities, along the way. Some sixty miles from here is a small city named Iconium. There is a synagogue there, I am told. Let us see what that might bring."

"How do you know there is a synagogue there?"

"I am from Tarsus. My father and others who were friends of my family traveled from Tarsus to Iconium."

"That was a long time ago."

"Correct. But the Jewish situation has not changed in Iconium. I know. I asked one of the Hebrews in Pisidia. And a traveling Greek merchant confirmed it. There is a synagogue in Iconium! It is the capital of the Galatian province of Lycaonia, and it is only sixty miles from here."

Barnabas raised one eyebrow. "Iconium it is. And thank you, Paul, for allowing me to know what we have decided to do."

"You are quite welcome, Barnabas. When we leave Iconium, feel free to ask me again."

"Fine. But at the first clean inn we come to, you must rest."

"No, we both must rest. You also have a criminal's back now!"

The two men turned south and east, into the heart of more Gentile country. The road was wide, the weather near perfect, and the land fertile. The road was dotted with homes and occasionally even a decent inn. In the far distance could be seen the Taurus Mountains.

On the fifth day of travel the two men came to a divide in the road. The Roman road signs showed that the left-hand road, heading slightly north, led to Iconium. The right-hand road, called the Sebaste Road, led south and east toward Lystra, Derbe, and eventually to Syria.

"Would you reconsider and take the right-hand lane, Paul? It will lead us home sooner."

"Let us take the left road. It is not far off our route. As the Lord allows, we will come back this way. Think of it, another city where the name of Jesus Christ has never been heard."

"I wonder what awaits us? Whip or rod?"

"Whichever, at least we don't have to wonder how it feels!"

And so my two friends turned left, toward Iconium.

CHAPTER 18

I came to Iconium just two years after Paul and Barnabas first arrived there.

What shall I tell you about Iconium? I have visited there twice. Situated in a valley, the walls of the city can be seen for miles before you arrive. It is a prosperous city, made so by the fertility of the plains that surround it. The local gods are Adonis and Cybele. The Jewish population is large. Should you happen to travel there, you will find Iconium to be a Greek-speaking town surrounded by a Latin-speaking world. Few Romans live there. The city lies between the regions of Phrygia and Lycaonia. A mountain range lies only six miles to the north. Two unusual peaks—the source of many fables—look down on the city.

Paul and Barnabas entered the city as inconspicuously as possible. They did not remain inconspicuous for long, however, and eventually they caused the biggest uproar in that city in a hundred years. Yet it all began so innocently. The two men made their way to a recommended inn and remained there awaiting the Sabbath. Rising early, they once more donned their respective Jewish attire and made their way to the synagogue. Again Paul was asked if he would like to speak. Paul, who grew up in a Greek city, stood. He spoke flawless Greek but changed to Hebrew and even gave a few quotations in Latin. All were impressed. There were God-fearing Gentiles present, all eager to hear Paul's words. Most would later become believers, as would a few Hebrews.

As before, the leaders of the synagogue soon became outraged that their building had been used by Hebrews to convert uncircumcised heathen to some spurious Jewish faith. And just as in Pisidia, the entire city soon heard of these men who declared that a god had died, come back alive, and forgiven men of their sins. But unlike in Pisidia, the city was divided from the very beginning. The marketplace saw at least one or two rousing arguments every day over the two men and their message.

During almost the entire four months Paul and Barnabas were in Iconium, they worked in the marketplace. In the mornings and evenings they gathered with the holy ones, who eventually became some fifty or sixty in number. About half were slaves; the rest were born free rather than having been freed. Regardless, the poverty was similar to other such places.

I have told you of the wonderful happenings in Antioch of Pisidia. The believers in Iconium experienced these same joys. Only they sang more, having a richer heritage in songs, as befits Greek people. The Iconians were every bit as exuberant in their faith as were the Pisidians.

Paul and Barnabas were very mindful of the relatively brief time they had been in Pisidia, so they deepened their messages in Iconium almost from the outset. They also warned the brothers and sisters that the two of them would probably not be with them very long. In light of this possibility, the two apostles shared very practical words along with their spiritual revelation.

One thing my two friends had learned was that these poor, illiterate Gentiles could grasp profound spiritual matters without knowing anything about Israel, the Hebrew religion, or anything else of Jewish ways.

Paul centered his message on nothing but Christ. Barnabas told stories of Christ and of the persecution and suffering in Judea, but he also added enthralling stories of what happened at Antioch of Pisidia. The Iconians loved it all and vowed that they would find a way to visit the holy ones in Pisidia. (Although Antioch is less than one hundred miles away, most had never heard of it. Such is the provincial nature of people who have to work out their existence on no more than the equivalent of fifty to a hundred denarii a year.)

Paul and Barnabas kept a sharp eye out for any travelers coming from Pisidia, hoping for a word about the believers there. Paul even hoped that one day a few of the believers in Pisidia might come to Iconium to give and receive encouragement.

It was a brother named Onesiphorus, a Greek, who opened his home as a place for the believers to gather. As the number of believers in Iconium grew, Onesiphorus was generous enough to tear out a wall to make room for a larger gathering.

Joy abounded. Like the Pisidians, Iconian believers were loud and boisterous, quick to laugh and quick to interrupt. Barnabas once commented, "In Galatia I interspersed a short message between two hours of interruptions." But do not misunderstand my words. The two men loved the Gentile way of gathering. These informal Gentiles helped Barnabas—and perhaps even Paul—to gain a deeper understanding of freedom in Christ. Two years later when I visited these Iconians, they set me free from chains I never even knew I was wearing.

Tension in the city soon mounted. By the fourth month it was obvious to all the believers that some kind of violence would soon erupt in their city. The leaders of the city were under much constraint by the synagogue leaders to take action against these two intruding foreigners. Hostility in the marketplace was also growing. Toward the end, Paul and Barnabas found it wise to stay out of the market entirely. There were rumors that the city fathers would look the other way if harm came to these troublemakers. This rumor did not escape the ears of some of the holy ones. Barnabas was quickly informed.

As Barnabas entered the room where he and Paul were staying, he said, "There are three ways of being thrown out of a city. We have experienced two of them. Let's not learn the third."

Paul looked up questioningly. His brow narrowed. "Whips and rods are two. What's the other?" he inquired.

"Stones."

"What . . . ?"

"There is a plot to stone us, my brother. It will come within hours."

"Who?"

"In Cyprus it was the *religious* world. In Pisidia it was the *civic* world. Here in Iconium it seems to be a mix of both." Paul was about to say something, but Barnabas continued. "We had better leave immediately."

The two men swept up their belongings, hid until dark, and then, by prearrangement, made their way to the home of one of the believers. For the next two nights they met with the assembly in clandestine gatherings. Then, in the hours just before dawn, they gathered with all the believers, as they had done in Pisidia. Every moment was packed with instructions, practical suggestions, and exhortations—all centered on Christ. The hours those men spent together were very serious times, yet always punctuated with lightheartedness.

One of the last things Barnabas suggested to the Lord's people was that they contact the Pisidian believers as soon as possible. Then he added, "Before we finally reach our own homeland, let us hope you will also have sister assemblies to the south and east as well as to the west."

Paul could not have been more pleased to hear his comrade speak such words. "Pray that a door will open in Lystra," added

Paul. "There is no synagogue there. That could be in our favor or against it. Either way, we have no clear means to find an audience with the citizens of that city."

Onesiphorus answered. "Here, more than in Pisidia, the Lord was with you in giving signs to his people. Through you, the Lord has healed many in our city who were diseased, blind, and at the point of death. Many in this room were added to the assembly because they saw these inexplicable wonders and were themselves the beneficiaries of these miracles. We shall ask Jesus to do the same for you in Lystra and in whatever city you choose to enter."

His words were simple, almost childlike, but they would influence Paul's method of operating in future days. And then the meeting ended in prayer. I have had the privilege of listening to those Iconians pray. I would that all men, especially those with religious backgrounds, could hear them. The words they spoke were honest, strikingly personal, and without any religious intonation or trite phrases.

The scene of their departure was not unlike that in Pisidia. During the night, accompanied by most of the brothers and sisters, Paul and Barnabas slipped out of Iconium. Once again, they left this small ecclesia with no scrolls, no leaders, and no building. Nor would these men come back for a long time.

The believers were rejected by their fellow citizens; they were poor, and virtually all were illiterate. Most were slaves, though some were freed men and a few were merchants. All had been godless heathen only four months before. It was this kind of people who said good-bye to the only two Christians they had ever known. But the power of the indwelling Holy Spirit had caused them to fall in love with Jesus Christ and then to love one another and care for one another.

Could such people survive, bereft of all outside help and with so little to offer one another? Probably we would have said it was impossible. I am sure we would have done so if we had known the crises they would face during the next several years. I still do not know how they survived! How could any community of believers survive what they went through? (I think even Barnabas and Paul might have agreed that their survival would be impossible under circumstances as grave as those they later passed through.) But that night hearts were light and full of hope as a hundred souls sang and shouted a boisterous good-bye.

By leaving Iconium that night, Barnabas and Paul just managed to escape violence. They would not be so fortunate in the next city.

CHAPTER 19

I have often heard Paul and Barnabas tell the story of what happened to them at the entrance gate to the city of Lystra. Of all that happened to them in their many adventures, this was always their favorite story. Every time I heard them tell it I laughed uncontrollably.

Lystra is about thirty miles south and west of Iconium and is situated on the banks of the Koprut River. If you visit this city, the first thing to catch your eye is a magnificent heathen temple immediately outside the city. This temple is dedicated to a god named Zeus and a man named Augustus Caesar. It is also this temple that got Paul and Barnabas in so much trouble. In fact, it almost cost Paul his life.

There are Romans in Lystra, but their number is small. This absence of a large Roman ruling class has allowed wealthy Greeks to control the city. But even they number only in the hundreds. There is no synagogue. Paul, therefore, knew he would not be able to employ his usual wedge into this city. The few Hebrews in Lystra worshiped only in a *proseuche*, that is, they met infrequently beside the Koprut River.

As Paul and Barnabas approached the city, the first oddity they noticed was the language. They understood not a single word anyone was saying, for they were hearing the local

Lycaonian dialect. This did not deter Paul. When they neared the city, he began preaching to a group of people in Greek. Even as he spoke he wondered if anyone would understand him. *I'm speaking to people who have never seen a Hebrew or even heard of one,* he thought. *This is truly heathen territory.*

One of those listening to Paul most intently was a cripple. It was at that moment that Paul remembered Onesiphorus's comment that signs and wonders had done much to add to the assembly in Iconium. "Stand up!" Paul said to the cripple. To the astonishment of everyone, the man jumped to his feet and started walking! It is of no small significance that this cripple had heard of the Jewish faith, truly feared God, and *believed* Paul. The crippled man was well known in Lystra, and when the crowd saw him walking, they began shouting in their local dialect. Paul and Barnabas had no idea what they were saying, but in typical fashion, Paul seized the moment. He looked intently at the cripple, took the man's hand, and began speaking again.

What Paul did not know—but every citizen in Lystra did— was an ancient Greek fable about this town. According to this legend, the god Zeus once came to Lystra, accompanied by the god Hermes. They knocked on the door of a thousand homes looking for lodging, but no one in the city showed them hospitality. Only one person, an old man named Philemon who lived in a straw hut outside town, opened his house to them. Philemon and his wife, Baucis, invited them in and offered them berries and cherries. Zeus and Hermes told the old man and woman to leave the city. They then covered the city with water but turned the old couple's *hut* into a *temple!* The legend also said Zeus would return to Lystra someday to test the people's hospitality again. In light of the miracle Paul had performed, the crowd concluded that Zeus and Hermes were *back!*

Messengers ran immediately to the temple of Zeus to notify the priests. Paul and Barnabas stood in the midst of all this commotion, wondering why people were rushing excitedly to the heathen temple while others fell prostrate at their feet.

Barnabas was horrified. People were bowing to him! He began bellowing his protest, which served only to convince the people even more that he was Zeus! Then, looking over toward the temple, Barnabas's confusion soared. Coming out of the temple were priests pulling a bull behind them. The priests, it turned out, were about to sacrifice the bull as an offering to them.

Finally realizing what was happening, my two Jewish friends reverted to one of their own native customs. A horrified Barnabas began tearing his clothes and throwing dirt in the air, wailing his protest. Paul joined him.

All this commotion virtually emptied the city. Everyone wanted to see Zeus—or laugh at those who wanted to! Paul, who had been wondering how he would ever find an audience in Lystra, had an entire city at his feet. The only problem was, they thought he was Hermes and wanted to worship him! Despite the language barrier, Paul called out, "Friends, why are you doing this? We are merely human beings like yourselves! We have come to bring you the Good News that you should turn from these worthless things"—Paul gestured toward the temple of Zeus—"and turn to the living God, who made heaven and earth, the sea, and everything in them. In earlier days he permitted all the nations to go their own ways, but he never left himself without a witness. There were always his reminders, such as sending you rain and good crops and giving you food and joyful hearts."

There were a few Greek merchants in the crowd, and they attempted to translate Paul's words. Finally the truth surfaced. The disappointed priests returned to the temple, and most of the people began to drift away.

In the crowd that day was an eighteen-year-old boy named Timothy. He was of mixed heritage, his father being Greek and his mother Jewish. Timothy, his mother, Eunice, and his grandmother Lois were almost the only people in the town fully familiar with Judaism. When Timothy heard Paul's message, he recognized that Paul and Barnabas were speaking of *his* God— the God he had known all his life through the stories his mother and grandmother had taught him from the Scriptures.

Timothy ran to find his mother. She, in turn, invited Paul and Barnabas to come to their home for dinner. This Jewish family was elated to hear that the Messiah had come, so they invited friends and relatives to come hear these visitors tell them about Jesus. A small group of new believers began to meet regularly in the small home of Eunice and her family. Eunice overflowed with praise that God had sent two men to this faraway region to tell them about the Messiah.

The gathering in Lystra was of a totally different culture than Iconium, just as Iconium's gatherings were different from those in the church in Antioch of Pisidia. The Christians in Lystra quickly developed a large repertoire of songs. Eunice and Lois knew many Hebrew psalms and quickly translated them into the Lycaonian language. Using the local folk music of Galatia to match the translated psalms, they developed an oral psalter for those who gathered.

Eunice introduced new songs with familiar melodies almost weekly. These people were illiterate, but they had strong memories. They sang the songs enthusiastically, but they also used the words to instruct and encourage one another in their meetings, which often lasted late into the night. I have had the privilege of meeting with these dear people. They stand and give strong words of encouragement to one another. Their closeness and care for one another are among the strongest I have ever known. Remarkably, Lystra is a poorer city than Iconium or Antioch, but the believers are no less knowledgeable in their living relationship with Christ.

You will be surprised to learn that the quietest, most unobserved person in the gatherings was our brother Timothy. He said *nothing*, and he stayed almost completely out of sight. Never once did he speak to Barnabas or Paul. They hardly knew he existed. Little did anyone realize how much and how well that youth was absorbing. Two years later, when he finally did speak out, it was as a volcano erupting.

Paul and Barnabas were able to stay in Lystra for about four months, preaching there and also in nearby villages. Unwittingly, they stayed too long. Word of their presence reached the ears of the leaders of the Hebrew synagogue in nearby Iconium. That proved to be disastrous. It was those very men who had succeeded in banishing Paul and Barnabas from Iconium. Now they were determined to see the same thing happen in Lystra.

The Jewish leaders in Antioch of Pisidia also heard this news, so they journeyed to Iconium to meet with the religious leaders in the synagogue to find a way to silence these meddling preachers. They were particularly outraged at hearing that so devout a Jew as Eunice had embraced Christ.

They devised a simple plan. Four men from Antioch and five from Iconium would travel to Lystra, go to the leading officials of the city, and warn them about these dangerous foreigners. The nine men vowed not to leave until they had turned Lystra against the visiting teachers. They succeeded in doing so with the city officials and then repeated their warnings to the Romans. Then they took their cares to the marketplace. Their interpretation of the events that had taken place in Antioch and Iconium made these two wanderers look like seditious revolutionaries and lying scoundrels.

With the leaders of the city on notice, the accusers turned to the priests of the temple of Zeus. Their impassioned words were successful, especially since the priests still felt foolish for having thought that Barnabas and Paul were gods. Soon a group of enraged men rushed to where Paul was working, grabbed him, and began to beat him. Someone threw a rock at him, and others followed suit. As Paul turned to escape, a rock hit him on the back of the head. He fell, unconscious. That rock may well have saved Paul's life, for his attackers thought that he was dead. Consequently, they threw their remaining rocks with less fury than at first. When they had finished their murderous work, they dragged Paul's body outside the city gates and left it crumpled in a ditch. With their work accomplished, the mob dispersed.

By that time, Eunice, Lois, and a few other believers had arrived on the scene. They cried out in grief as they saw Paul's bruised and bleeding body lying motionless beside the road. They stood in horror, not sure what to do.

Barnabas arrived and knelt down beside his friend. He put his cheek against Paul's bloodied lips to see if there was any sign of breath. "Paul? Paul, can you hear me? Are you alive?"

A muffled groan escaped Paul's lips. "The rock throwers, are they gone?"

"Paul! You're alive! Yes, they're gone." Barnabas cradled Paul's head and began to wipe the blood from his face. "Don't try to move, Paul. You're badly hurt."

"Yes, it hurts," Paul whispered hoarsely, "but I can't let them think they've killed me." Paul then sat up, gingerly touching the wounds on his head. It was as though he had risen from the dead. To his friends, who thought he *was* dead, he might just as well have been resurrected. His face was cut, swollen, bruised, and streaked with blood. His clothes were torn, and he was covered with dust and blood from head to foot, but he was alive! Terror and joy mingled together in everyone's heart. It was at that moment that Paul truly showed his indomitable spirit. He struggled to his feet, trying unsuccessfully to smile through cracked lips. "Well, Barnabas, we've experienced the whip, rods, and now stones. That about covers it, doesn't it?"

Barnabas smiled with relief. "Well, there's always the blade."

"Yes, but there is no surviving that one," managed Paul.

Although his enemies thought they had succeeded in silencing him, Paul insisted on returning to the city. So Barnabas and the others helped him back to Eunice's home, where Paul bathed his wounds and rested for a while. Although he could hardly move, Paul then called for a meeting of the entire assembly! They quickly gathered in Eunice's front room, and Paul talked to them all through the night. Finally, as dawn's pink glow began to lighten the eastern sky, Paul and Barnabas prayed with their dear friends. Then, accompanied by all the believers, they left the city. As they passed the spot where Paul had been so unceremoniously dumped just hours before, they waved good-bye and set out toward Derbe. One of those who walked with them to the city gates that morning was Timothy, still the quiet watcher.

Paul and Barnabas had been in Lystra less than five months. They had arrived in a pagan city, where the name of Jesus had never been heard and only a handful of Jews knew the living God, the God of creation. Yet they left a vibrant church, an ecclesia of believers who cared for one another and delighted to worship their Lord in song and word. To this day I am enthralled by the thought that these two men could plant the gathering of Christ and do it so well in so short a time. And then they dared to *leave*. Granted, they had little alternative, but they left a young, uneducated, unlettered, and leaderless people. Yet they left with confidence that the ecclesia would not only survive but also grow in the Lord.

And remember, all the fury of Satan broke out upon this church just two years later. How they survived that savage onslaught I have no way to tell.

❦

Half walking, half limping, with Barnabas at his side, Paul was able to travel a few miles that first day. The two men spent the night at an inn, then pushed on toward Derbe. One more assembly waited to be planted by these two intrepid planters of churches.

Derbe lies some sixty miles east of Lystra. Its only distinction is that Antipater (friend of Cicero) was born there. Should you visit Derbe, be advised that there is only one inn there. The ecclesia is small, and the people are unbelievably poor.

The assembly in Derbe can be remembered as the easternmost church Paul ever planted. Had he wished to do so, Paul could easily have passed by Derbe and continued on to his native city, Tarsus. He certainly had every reason to consider doing so, for he was a physical disaster; but of a truth, no such thought entered his mind.

The planting of the church in Derbe was the only one that knew no violence. No persecution was experienced. As a result, the two men could have remained in Derbe for a long time (as some today do), but they had observed that God, in his sovereign use of circumstances, had allowed them to stay no more than five months in the other three cities. They took this as God's plan: four to five months in a city. Raise up and leave a church in the space of less than half a year. Paul followed this plan throughout most of his ministry. That amazing fact holds me in awe to this very day.

It was in Derbe that our beloved brother Gaius became a believer. Some seven years later, Gaius became one of the eight young men Paul trained to continue the Lord's work among the heathen after he was gone. Paul called these men out of several churches to accompany him to plant churches. Gaius, Timothy, and the others later planted churches among the heathen in other lands. But that took place long after the Galatian story. In fact, it is the story of what happened in Ephesus.

While Paul and Barnabas were in Derbe, brothers from all four churches began meeting one another. The feast of Bacchus was celebrated annually throughout all Galatia. Taking advantage of that week of festivities, two brothers from Antioch of Pisidia set out to visit Paul and Barnabas and the young ecclesia in Derbe. Of course, they visited Iconium along the way, so four

brothers from Iconium decided to accompany them to Derbe.
The six men turned east at the juncture of the Augustan Road
and the Sebaste Road. The saints in Lystra heard about all this,
so they rented a wagon and sent five men to join the group as
they passed through Lystra on their way to Derbe. Just before
the wagonload of eleven brothers arrived at Derbe on the third
day of the festival, the entire assembly, having heard of their
approach, came out to meet them. For the first time, the
believers in Derbe were meeting brothers from the other three
assemblies. The others had known one another for only a few
days, but they talked all day and almost all night, sharing stories
and adventures of their respective ecclesias. They laughed,
cheered, and exhorted one another. Finally, as the heathen wine
festival neared its conclusion, they knelt, prayed, wept, and
bade one another good-bye.

I have heard some of the holy ones in Derbe say that it was
the greatest moment of their lives. All four Galatian churches
were strengthened.

Although none of them realized it at the time, something
very important happened during that visit. It was a simple thing,
but later it proved to be of extreme importance. As a result of
this meeting of believers from all the Galatian churches, there
were now brothers from all four ecclesias who had met *Timothy*.
Two years later that simple fact played a major role in the
survival of all four churches.

Just before the wagon departed Derbe, Paul and Barnabas
announced that they would soon be returning home to Antioch
of Syria. The brothers from Iconium and Pisidia urged them to
choose a route home that would bring them back through their
cities. The two apostles were reluctant. It would be closer to
continue eastward by land, and both men, remembering the
shipwreck, wanted to go home by land rather than by sea.
There was also another problem: They were outlaws in Pisidia
and Iconium, and they were hated in Lystra. But the brothers

from Iconium and Pisidia spoke so enthusiastically about their visiting that they relented. Then the brothers began to discuss how to *smuggle* Paul and Barnabas into their towns. Paul was wary about ever entering Lystra again, but after listening to the plans for just such a possibility, he could not help but agree. "But this time, make sure it's Barnabas who receives any stones as gifts from the good citizens of Lystra," he added.

"If we get out of Lystra alive, I plan to carry a stone with me to show to the ecclesia in Antioch of Syria," said Barnabas.

"One *without* any of my blood on it," rejoined Paul.

∞

Nearly two years had now passed since Paul and Barnabas had departed from Syria. Both looked forward to home and rest, even though Derbe itself had proven to be the beginning of a time of healing. During all that time, however, Paul had never fully recovered from his many ordeals.

After about four months in Derbe, the two men began their journey home by retracing their steps through Lystra, Iconium, and Antioch of Pisidia. Paul had been fully assured of his safe return through all three cities. What he really dreaded now was repeating that long, dangerous sea journey from Perga to Syria.

As Paul and Barnabas left Derbe, they waved a fond and loving farewell to the members of the body of Christ in that city.

Five days later, about ten miles from Lystra, they saw a wagon loaded with grain coming toward them. As planned, the two men climbed aboard and buried themselves in the cargo. The wagon then turned around and headed toward Lystra.

When Barnabas told this story, he often commented, "We arrived in Lystra disguised as a loaf of bread." Paul's only comment was, "I prefer a Damascus basket."

For a week the two men met with the holy ones in Lystra but always in the dead of night. The two rejoiced to see how the church in Lystra had grown in size and in the believers' understanding of Christian love. They prayed together and read the Scriptures (Barnabas still had his precious scrolls with him). They had no way of knowing if they would ever see each other again, so Paul and Barnabas gave them instructions on many diverse subjects.

But Paul and Barnabas learned as much or more from the churches as the churches did from them. (Certainly that has been true in my own life.) In each town, the two brothers saw a whole new way that the ecclesia could be expressed. That unique, local, and varied expression had come into being because each had been left on its own to discover its own natural way of functioning as the body of Christ. When left alone, the brothers met almost every day, and the sisters also met together. The entire body also gathered frequently for no purpose except to be together. Other times they met to plan future meetings— often to do no more than eat together. And laugh together.

All participated, and there was endless variety. They had learned well what they had heard of expressing Christ. As a result, a fresh, new ecclesia emerged in each of the four cities, each unique from the others. Further, they were unlike anything this world had ever seen.

In Christ there is no such thing as Jew or Gentile, wealthy or poor, male or female. And in these gatherings of the body of Christ, the slaves who have met Christ are the freest of all the people in the world.

Their meetings, all made up of people who had been heathen just a few months before, were always full of joy, laughter, sharing, spontaneous singing, and interruptions . . . always interruptions.

∞

Just before leaving Lystra, Paul and Barnabas surprised everyone by appointing a few men as elders, or guardians, in case the church experienced a major crisis and needed such leaders.

"What are the elders to do?" they inquired.

"Very little, we hope!" responded Barnabas. "They, and all of you, hopefully, will continue on as you are. But if there is a crisis, if there are major uncertainties, if there is very serious confusion, look to these men. Otherwise, continue as you are."

Rather than depart Lystra the same way they arrived, buried in grain, the two men waited until midnight and calmly walked out the city's gates, kicking the stone steps of the temple of Zeus with their sandals as they passed by.

Barnabas, as he said he would, picked up a stone, put it in his satchel, and carried it all the way home to Syria. Paul thought poorly of the idea and didn't disguise his contempt for that particular stone.

There was far more danger in daring to enter Iconium than Lystra, for the two had been officially banished from that city. They were considered criminals. To be discovered inside the city would cost them a life of imprisonment or even death.

As at Derbe, the brothers from Iconium came out to meet them. They dressed the two apostles in the garb of wandering Greek philosophers and waited for darkness. Then, accompanied by two Roman soldiers who were believers, the entire troop walked boldly into Iconium.

All meetings were held in the deep of night. Here, as in Lystra, the Holy Spirit chose elders, men who were reluctant to lead but who had the confidence of the other holy ones if a crisis arose. Paul and Barnabas spent only five days in Iconium, for they were keenly aware that their presence would soon be known if they stayed longer.

A large number of brothers accompanied Paul and Barnabas out of Iconium and all the way to Antioch of Pisidia. A close bond had grown up between these two ecclesias, despite the long distance that separated them.

As this band of men neared Antioch, a wagon approached. It was empty except for one brother, who was driving the horses. For a moment the apostles were confused as to how an empty wagon could get them safely through the gates and into the city. But just a few moments after the arrival of the wagon, other brothers began to appear as from nowhere. Within an hour over twenty men had met them on the road. That night Paul and Barnabas went through the gates of Antioch of Pisidia crammed in the center of a wagon loaded with twenty men, all trying to look very solemn but struggling hard not to laugh.

As they had done in Lystra and Iconium, Paul and Barnabas encouraged the believers in Antioch to continue in the faith, reminding them that they must enter into the kingdom of God through many tribulations. Paul and Barnabas also appointed elders and prayed for them with fasting, turning them over to the care of the Lord, in whom they had come to trust.

After a week of much encouragement and strengthening that came to all and from all, the two weary sojourners began making preparations for that treacherous journey out of Galatia, down the plateau, and into the lowlands of Pamphylia. Their destination was the town of Perga and the nearby seaport village of Attalia. Dread filled both men's hearts as they looked at the road. They could think only of robbers, rain, snow, floods, sleeping in forests, and filthy inns. But the holy ones from all four of the ecclesias had thought of better things. Together they gave their apostles a most wonderful and most appreciated gift.

For two months the holy ones in Derbe, Lystra, and Iconium had been saving their grain, chickens, and vegetables. Then they bartered all this for a few silver coins, which they sent to the believers in Antioch of Pisidia by way of the brothers from Iconium. The saints in Antioch had also managed to barter their saved grain for two additional silver coins. With these coins the brothers in Antioch bought passage for Paul and Barnabas to Perga: two seats on a wagon that would be accompanied by a garrison of Roman soldiers! There was even enough silver left over to allow them to buy food and lodging at the inns along the way.

As Paul and Barnabas marveled at this generosity, the brothers who had arranged for their fare reminded them of the standard instructions: "You get to ride in the wagon as long as the ground is level. For the safety of both wagon and horses, no one rides in the wagon going up or down a hill!"

One bright morning more than one hundred brothers and sisters emerged from Antioch of Pisidia, singing and shouting good-byes to their dearly loved church planters. Paul and Barnabas ended their work in Galatia amongst songs, praises, cheers, and shouted prayers. "A group of believers from a city called Antioch sent us off in the first place with joy and singing. The believers from another Antioch are sending us back home in the same fashion," observed Barnabas.

Barnabas could not help but eye the curious soldiers who had never seen slaves smiling, much less crying out for joy. From that moment and throughout the entire journey, the soldiers treated the two men with an extra measure of respect.

When the caravan reached the place where the bridge had been washed out, Paul and Barnabas dismounted the wagon, knelt, and thanked their Lord for his caring hand and for *all* that had happened after that horrible day. Later they rode in silence past the place where they had witnessed the beatings of their two Greek traveling companions.

They tried to identify places where they had slept in the woods and the place where the flood had almost caught them. But all had changed. It was spring, the days were bright, the weather warm, and the fields verdant, not to mention the absence of robbers in the presence of Roman swords.

At last our two brothers arrived back in Perga, there to report to the beloved saints and to rejoice with them in all that

God had done. They stayed longer than they had intended, for few ships were sailing from Attalia to Antioch of Syria. (Paul and Barnabas refused to sail first to Cyprus. "Antioch or nowhere," they said, "and certainly not another trip to Cyprus.") Eventually, however, they found passage on a large freighter bound directly for Antioch's harbor, Seleucia.

Sitting in Ahira's home, the brothers and sisters in Perga had listened to Paul and Barnabas's story and received it with great delight. After hearing about the four new churches, they were determined to go up to Galatia and meet their new brothers and sisters.

Since that time, every year in late summer or early fall, a large group of holy ones from Perga joins a caravan and goes to Pisidia to spend a week with the holy ones meeting in Galatia. On occasion some of the brothers and sisters from the Galatian churches have also come down to meet with the believers in Perga. As a result of all this, the Perga assembly began to lean more toward the Gentile churches than toward the more staid Hebrew gatherings on Cyprus. Today the ecclesia in Perga is mostly Gentile in makeup, I am told.

⚭

What did my two friends accomplish during their two years' travel?

First, they changed the very direction of the faith. There were now Gentile believers and Gentile churches. And those ecclesias were like nothing else on earth. *Beyond compare.* Their gatherings were unlike those of any other believers in all the world. These dear Galatian souls knew virtually nothing of Hebrew traditions or even of Jewish history. They are, I tell you, truly unique. The way they love, the way they care, and the way they carry on their meetings simply cannot be explained. It must be witnessed.

Under the sovereignty of God, the churches in the central

part of Asia Minor had been planted within reach of the churches in the western part of Cilicia. Paul and Barnabas never realized the significance of that fact, but the geographic proximity of those Gentile churches later saved the lives of countless Jewish believers when they fled their homeland in Israel! God was working in ways none of us then knew. Nor could we have understood.

While Paul and Barnabas were in Galatia, the brothers and sisters in Antioch of Syria had begun to reach out and plant churches in cities north and west of Antioch. Eventually, the northernmost of these churches was not too far from Derbe! A small event, one might think, but thousands of Jewish brothers fleeing Judea had to follow this very route. As they moved north toward the small province of Asia, these Jews were cared for by the uncircumcised Gentile believers in northern Syria—and in *Galatia!*

What else had these men done? They had proven that poor, illiterate people, without buildings or books—believers meeting in living rooms and without even a copy of the Hebrew Scriptures—could know an indwelling Lord and love that Lord as well as anyone.

In a word, four churches existed wholly outside the Jewish community. This, as we shall see, set off a firestorm.

CHAPTER 20

Before leaving Galatia, Barnabas had written a letter to the church in Antioch of Syria to tell the holy ones there that he and Paul were alive and had at last turned homeward. But letters written to distant places often never arrived, and so it was in this case. The assembly there had no idea Paul and Barnabas were coming home. When the two men arrived at the seaport of Seleucia, no one was there to greet them. The two men trekked the sixteen miles to Antioch alone and in silence, wondering what their unexpected arrival might do. "They don't even know we are alive," murmured Barnabas.

Walking into Antioch and onto the broad central street, they looked everywhere for a familiar face. Finally, a young brother did see them. A moment of astonishment was followed by a shout of glee. "Barnabas and Paul are home! Alive! Safe and in high spirits."

As the news of their homecoming flew through the city, everyone wanted to know, "When can we see them? When can we hear from them?"

By now the assembly in Antioch numbered in the thousands and was the second largest ecclesia in the empire. For that reason the church rarely attempted to gather all together in one place. Naturally, such meetings were always eagerly anticipated, and they were times of great refreshment and thunder-ous praise.

Finding a place for all the believers to gather is always a problem in Antioch. One of the slaves, Dora by name, was a confidante of her mistress owner, who was departing for a visit to Rome. As she had done several times in the past, this wealthy Roman lady agreed to allow all the believers to gather in the garden behind her home, a villa perched on one of the hills just outside the city.

The meeting began three hours before dawn, with torches placed along the garden wall. I am told it was a beautiful scene. Barnabas and Paul arrived early, hugging everyone in sight as they passed through the crowd. The first song seemed to shake the earth. Someone reminded them to quiet down lest they waken the wealthy neighbors; nonetheless, shouts of joy rose to the skies as Barnabas stood to speak.

Barnabas spoke for three hours, bringing everyone to tears (as well as peals of laughter) and finally to a wild ovation. Paul spoke only for a few minutes, mostly clarifying some of his friend's comments, as Barnabas had concentrated on telling Paul's exploits. It was understood that Paul would speak the next morning. The meeting ended in a song that wafted out over the city of Antioch.

The next morning, again before dawn, Paul held the believers in awe for four hours. Then questions began. Barnabas joined Paul as both added stories to the questions.

"It felt so good to be home," Paul remarked to me.

The meeting ended about noon, with a meal served in the woods just above the villa. Many remained until evening, listening, sharing, and telling the two men all that had happened in Syria during their two-year absence.

A deep satisfaction entered everyone's heart. When the church in Antioch had sent these two men out under the direction of the Holy Spirit, everything had worked together for good to the glory of Jesus Christ. Their Lord had been proclaimed among the Gentiles in places where he had never been known. One brother spoke for all when he said, "Not since the coming of Moses has such a thing been known among the heathen nations. And we played a part in it!" The unclean had heard the gospel and responded with great joy.

∞

During the coming months Paul and Barnabas rested. Paul's full recovery came slowly and with many setbacks. To allow rest for his friend, Barnabas pursued his new skill of leather crafting in Antioch's marketplace.

It did not go unnoticed among the holy ones that their two church planters were capable of a rare gift—the ability *to lay aside their ministry*. For more than a year, both men simply took their place in the daily life of the ecclesia, no more conspicuous than the simplest of brothers. They did not expect special treatment, and they did not appear to be men who for two years had been like lions.

Word soon reached the church in Jerusalem that Barnabas and Paul had planted four churches in Galatia—and that none of those Gentile believers had been circumcised. The reaction was quite mixed. Some received it with joy, while others felt that Barnabas and Paul had committed a heresy that would lead to terrible consequences. I know! I was living in the holy city at the time the news reached Jerusalem.

Some within the household of God in Jerusalem began to attack Barnabas. "Why was Barnabas sent to Antioch of Syria? He was sent to Antioch to evaluate the situation and report back to the Twelve. Now there is a so-called church in Antioch that has become mostly Gentile. And look what happened next! We hear stories of his going to Galatia and raising up other so-called churches, accompanied by a man who may not even be a true believer. Worse, some dare call these men "apostles." We hear that the Antioch believers don't even attend the synagogue services! Barnabas should return here to Jerusalem and give account of his unauthorized actions."

Why did Barnabas seek out a renegade Jewish convert from a Gentile city to help him in Antioch? As some saw it, Barnabas, Paul, and the ecclesia in Antioch had produced disastrous results for the kingdom of God. Further, without consulting Peter, they had even dared to wander off into the very heart of the poorest, vilest, most unclean region of heathendom and had allowed uncircumcised Gentile infidels to follow the Jewish Messiah.

The men who spoke this way surmised that Barnabas had deliberately disobeyed Peter. Personally, I think they deliberately sought to spread doubt about Barnabas.

The leader of this party of criticism was an incredibly gifted man who had great influence in Jerusalem. It was this very man who eventually demanded that Peter go to this renegade ecclesia in Syria and stop these two false "apostles."

Many of the people in the Jerusalem church did not know about these accusations and rumblings, for the ringleaders directed most of what they said to Peter and the other apostles. Peter was, after all, the key to the direction the gospel would take. So these men demanded of Peter that Barnabas, Paul, Antioch, and Galatia be brought under the wings of the Jerusalem assembly. They also demanded that this "new" gospel be stopped, that the churches in Galatia be corrected, and that their practices be changed. "And all these unclean heathen must be circumcised," they added emphatically.

They left Peter no other choice but to do *something*. "Reprimand these men. Change these churches. If they refuse to be changed, renounce them."

Peter showed little interest in these men's concerns, but he did not want to see the Jerusalem church brought into a major controversy. That church had suffered enough. Peter's visit to the home of Cornelius and his vision concerning all things being clean had profoundly affected him. Nonetheless, our brother Peter could at times be inordinately affected by pressures that were placed on him.

Peter turned to some of the brothers for counsel, and they suggested that Peter go to Antioch and see everything firsthand. Peter agreed.

We have come now to that point in the Galatian story that has caused so much controversy among the churches: *What happened when Peter was in Antioch?* What later caused Paul to write so radical a letter as he did to the four churches in Galatia?

To bring an end to these misunderstandings, I will now tell you what really happened in Antioch and what unbelievable things happened in Galatia.

CHAPTER 21

 P eter is coming! Peter, the Lord's first apostle, is coming to Antioch!" It was the most exciting news the church in Antioch had ever received. Paul and Barnabas were elated—and worried.

The church in Jerusalem was made up mostly of Jews who had become believers in Jesus as the Messiah. As a result, the ecclesia there was Jewish in culture. Paul knew that some of the leaders in Jerusalem were skeptical about the very idea of Gentiles becoming believers—unless they first converted to Judaism. He wondered whether Peter would accept the Gentile believers as true brothers and sisters in Christ.

Barnabas was also concerned but for a different reason. Peter had been Barnabas's mentor. It was hard not to like Peter. He was the natural leader of all the saints. He had great power from God, he had a ready wit, and the Lord had obviously chosen him to lead. And lead he did. Barnabas looked at Peter as the man who gave him Christ. Barnabas loved Peter and greatly respected him.

But there was a problem. "Some of the believers in Jerusalem think that my work with you Gentiles here in Antioch is an act of disobedience. Still, Peter had plenty of time to censure me, and he never did. He might have instructed me by letter.

He never did. To my knowledge Peter has never spoken an unkind word about Antioch nor about what I have done here."

These were Barnabas's words—and his hopes—as he sought to explain to the brothers in Antioch what Peter's coming might mean. He was rightly apprehensive, for despite Barnabas's high hopes, many Pharisees and scribes in the church in Jerusalem were opposed to the Antioch assembly. They had little good to say of Barnabas, and even less of brother Paul.

The Antioch brothers listened to Barnabas's comment and were not at all surprised to hear that Paul was still a source of controversy in Judea. That fact was well known, though it was usually mentioned in good humor among the believers in Antioch.

Paul had a response: "I do not believe Peter sees Barnabas's actions as an act of disobedience. Negligence, perhaps, but not disobedience." Paul's comment drew laughter. Then he added, "When Peter comes and sees the Holy Spirit among you and finds that you are men and women who live by divine life, he will see the will of God concerning the Gentiles."

Despite Paul's words, and despite the joy flowing through the assembly because of Peter's impending arrival, there was a certain apprehension in the air. The Gentiles wanted desperately to be received as brothers by the assemblies in Judea, for they knew they *were* brothers.

Paul urged them, "Regardless of what people say, never forget how perfectly Jesus Christ has chosen you and received you."

Peter's arrival was unforgettable. Brothers had waited on the side of the road outside of Antioch for two days. Upon seeing Peter and his company walking toward them, one brother quickly rode a horse back to the city to announce that Peter was only a few miles away. As planned, virtually everyone in the Antioch ecclesia rushed out to greet Peter.

Seeing Peter in the distance, they all began to sing to him.

Peter was overjoyed. As one who knows him, it is not hard for me to imagine what he did. Peter began running toward them, crying, "Christians, Christians," a name that the unbelievers in Antioch had given to the believers. Until that moment, the believers had never known exactly how to react to being called "Christians." But hearing Peter call them Christians (a name they did not realize he even knew), it suddenly became a compliment rather than an insult.

The brothers and sisters exploded with laughter and rushed toward him with shouts of joy. Suddenly Peter was engulfed by a thousand people calling out greetings and throwing flowers at him. Peter was wholly taken in by the believers in Antioch. There was not one moment thereafter (until the arrival of the Pharisees from Jerusalem) that Peter uttered even one word of criticism to anyone. It was love, unbounded love, on all sides. I repeat: Until the Pharisees from Jerusalem arrived, Peter never uttered one negative word about Antioch.

Early every morning Peter preached to the assembly. They also met in the evenings, for in Antioch it is safe to be out on the streets. (Antioch is perhaps the only great city on earth where this is true—for the great avenues of the city are lit every night by torches.) Peter proved to be a storyteller without peer. He entertained the holy ones with stories of his time with Jesus, the persecution in Jerusalem, and the birth of the many churches in Judea and Galilee. And he managed always to make himself the goat of every story.

"I am the most hugged man on earth," he said one night, commenting on the Gentiles' unrestrained way of expressing their affection.

But it was when Peter began praying for the sick that the whole city was stirred. The number of those added to the Lord grew each week. The assembly's love for Peter and their respect for him grew without bounds.

Let it be said here that when Simon Peter was in Antioch,

he was given full freedom to do whatever he desired, to say what he desired, and to lead the church in any way he desired. Still, he gave not a word of correction. Everything he said and did spoke of total acceptance. Let it be known, too, that there were many new converts in Antioch while Peter was there, and not one was circumcised.

After Peter had been in Antioch for six weeks, he announced he would travel up the coast of Syria (toward Cilicia) and visit the new churches in that region. He would take Barnabas and Paul and be gone for about a month. His purpose was to strengthen, comfort, and encourage those young ecclesias, heal the sick, and proclaim Christ to the nonbelievers.

I have always believed it was the providence of God that Peter made this journey, for he was not in Antioch when the Pharisees arrived. (They arrived in Antioch just after Peter left.)

It is important that you understand what happened next.

CHAPTER 22

News of Peter's arrival in Antioch and his exuberant reaction to the Gentile believers made its way back to Jerusalem. The scribes, priests, and Pharisees in the Jerusalem ecclesia were opposed to Antioch, and they did not like this latest news. So a group of these Pharisees set out for Antioch!

One of these men was the brilliant leader mentioned earlier. He was a man of great influence in Jerusalem. I have never met anyone quite like him. You have probably never heard any mention of him, but that's because Paul later made a decision never to speak of this man and never to warn the churches of his coming. In fact, I was with Paul on the very day he made that decision. This man became the avowed enemy of Paul, but you will find no reference to him in Paul's writings.

Of whom do I speak? The infamous Blastinius Drachrachma. He was the Pharisee who led that company of Pharisees and scribes to Antioch.

Before leaving Jerusalem, Blastinius went to James, the brother of Jesus, and told James he would be traveling to Antioch to visit the holy ones. He then requested a letter of introduction and commendation from James to the church in Antioch, a customary gesture when a member from one body visits another. So the letter of introduction was written.

Did James himself actually sign the letter? To this day I do not know. It was a point never clarified. (I *believe* James signed it but had no idea how Blastinius would use it to cause such enormous damage among the Gentiles.)

Upon obtaining the letter, Blastinius departed for Antioch, taking with him seven other men, all Pharisees or scribes. They were the most zealous men for the law of Moses in the ecclesia in Jerusalem.

It is difficult to describe Blastinius. He was tall and skinny. His face was stern. But therein lies the enigma. When necessary, he could appear warm and understanding. He could turn any discussion to his advantage without ever seeming stern. He always sat erect. He rarely spoke during ordinary conversations. Most of the time he was silent. But when he spoke on subjects of his interest, he had no peer. He spoke slowly. He had an uncanny ability to make even an ordinary comment sound like a profound commentary. Consequently, people clung to his every word. Although he was devoid of all humor, he had many followers. I never met anyone so fanatically possessed with the Jewish law. His iron will made him the very essence of one who believed that all men should obey the entire law—and that one could actually be successful in such a pursuit. He could make every man who listened to him believe that the law *could* be obeyed and *must* be obeyed. Most of all, Blastinius was determined to bend the will of all other men to his, and he had the gift to do so.

Blastinius was so angry when he saw the "so-called church" (his words) in Antioch that he made a vow to God to follow Paul all the rest of his life and do all in his power to destroy Paul's ministry. Wherever Paul planted a church, Blastinius would follow him and teach it to obey the law of Moses. And if he could not persuade those assemblies to turn to the law, he would destroy them. Blastinius was that obsessed. He lived and breathed for the utter destruction of a Gentile gospel and all the

Gentile ecclesias. The pursuit possessed him. Unfortunately, he was the one man in Israel who had the ability to do just what he intended to do.

Paul had known Blastinius years earlier when both sat under the great teacher Gamaliel. Paul himself was a zealot of the Jewish traditions in those days, but even he was unnerved by the controlling bent and charismatic nature of Blastinius.

So Blastinius came to Antioch, bringing with him a glowing letter of introduction from James and the church in Jerusalem. He arrived the day after Paul, Barnabas, and Peter had left to travel north. The church in Antioch, though it did not know it, was now at the mercy of a man who possessed the magnetism of Peter and the insights of Paul. If you can understand this man, you can understand what really happened in Galatia. Then you will understand why Paul later wrote that controversial letter to the four churches in Galatia.

We come to the drama that was to shock all the churches— that famous and dramatic confrontation between Paul and Peter in Antioch and the equally famous confrontation in Jerusalem.

CHAPTER 23

The church in Antioch of Syria threw open its arms to Blastinius. Within a few days Blastinius had won over the church in Antioch. His beguiling ways, his piety, his wisdom, and his demeanor were appealing to all those with religious inclinations who met him. (Unfortunately, he was not the last man to be so endowed.)

The assembly in Antioch felt especially blessed to have received another important guest from the ecclesia in Jerusalem. They were certain they had found full acceptance from the Hebrew believers. Blastinius and his friends were soon speaking in the twenty or thirty houses where the ecclesia gathered.

Blastinius began his teaching with an emphasis on the prophecies in the Hebrew Scripture that spoke of a coming Messiah. Everyone loved it. Gradually he moved toward the need for obedience to the laws and ordinances of Moses. This was his first step toward his conclusion that obedience to circumcision was essential. His incisive words, his piety, his intellect won everyone over without their even noticing.

For one full month Blastinius held forth in Antioch. Whenever Peter's name came up, Blastinius was lavish with praise. But he spoke only with condescension of Barnabas. And he spoke not a word when Paul's name was mentioned. His silence was powerful. He managed to place doubt in the hearts of almost everyone concerning Paul, yet without uttering a single word to that end. Such was the power of Blastinius.

During that entire time, Peter was traveling north. He had said he would be returning to Jerusalem soon after his trip to northern Syria, so the believers in Antioch planned a great farewell feast for him. Everyone in the ecclesia would be there to honor Peter.

In the meantime, Blastinius had reached the point where he felt he could demand that the uncircumcised be circumcised. That is exactly what he did, and this immediately set off a controversy. The church was thrown into confusion. A few days longer and the church might have been divided.

It was at this moment that Peter and Barnabas returned. (Paul had tarried in one of the churches north of Antioch.) As soon as Blastinius learned that Peter was back in Antioch, he demanded a meeting with him. All day and late into the night, Blastinius and his company pressed Peter concerning the teachings of the law. Peter was shaken. So was Barnabas. So also were the other Antioch believers in the room.

Paul arrived in Antioch the next morning, the day of the farewell banquet for Peter. Paul was immediately sought out by the brothers in Antioch. "Leaders have come from the church in Jerusalem, Paul. They have been teaching us things we have never known. They were sent by James, the very brother of the Lord Jesus. Is what they say true?"

Paul became perfectly still. His face was ashen. "From James?" his voice cracked with emotion.

"Yes."

"Who are they, these teachers who came while we were gone? Is it John? any of the Twelve? Are there any Pharisees?"

"Not the Twelve."

Paul was relieved. "Then who?"

"The leader, the one who has taught everyone, is named Blastinius Drachrachma."

Paul grabbed his forehead and began to shake. One of the believers standing near Paul heard him whisper, "Lord, no. Deliver me from such a man."

Pulling himself together, Paul said, "Sit down. Let me hear it all."

All morning and into the early afternoon Paul listened to the brothers tell what the last month had held. One thing was clear. Every man in the room was afraid. It was as though the foundation of their lives was crumbling.

"I look at your faces. I see in them something I have never seen before." He paused. "At least not among the Gentiles."

"What?"

"Guilt. A sense of guilt. A sense of inadequacy. A sense of unworthiness. That you feel you are of lower rank than others in God's kingdom. That Jerusalem is more Christian than Antioch!" Paul jutted out his jaw and then bit off every word he uttered. "Such is the power of the law!

"Any man who places his hope in obedience to the law will forever feel inadequate, always feeling he must strive harder to please God. He will forever be uncertain as to whether God is pleased with him. How do I know this? I have *tried*. So has Peter. So has Barnabas. We all ended up with an overwhelming sense of *failure*. Now, in the midst of the freedom you have received from Christ, there has appeared an old and impossible gospel. It is "good news" that is not good news at all. Shall we who know God's highest . . . shall we return to something that never gave us hope?"

"It is time for the farewell meal with Peter," observed one of the brothers. "It begins shortly."

"Are they still here? Will they be at the dinner?"

"Yes, but they won't eat with us!"

Paul's eyes blazed. "Oh, I see! That's because *you* are

second-class believers. You are less important than God's Hebrew children. You are nothing but poor, unclean, uncircumcised heathen! How dare you think you are worthy to sit with a
son of Abraham! How dare you think that you could sit with
Blastinius Drachrachma!"

The brothers were stunned. Then, as they understood
Paul's sarcasm, they suddenly understood what Blastinius had
done to them.

"I have two questions," Paul barked. "Have any of you
yielded to circumcision?"

"No. We had some very long meetings about this. We
finally decided to wait until Peter returned so we could ask him
what we should do."

"Wait for Peter!" Paul exclaimed, rising to his feet. "And
who is Paul?! Are we lesser apostles than Peter? Is the gospel
defined by man?" The room fell silent. No one had ever seen
Paul so angry.

"My next question: Has Peter ever refused to eat with you,
ever, while he has been here?"

"No."

"But Blastinius has?"

"Yes!" came the response of a brother who was gradually
awakening to greater confidence.

"Did you feel shame because he did not eat with you? Did
you feel inferior?"

For a long moment there was silence. Finally one brother
answered, "That's exactly how I felt."

"But never again," said another, his voice strong.

Without another word, Paul left the room, his eyes blazing.

Today, so many years later, our brother Paul is remembered
mostly for two things: One is what he said to Peter that afternoon; the other is what he wrote in his letter to the four
churches in Galatia. You might think those two actions were
characteristic of Paul, but just the opposite is true. Those were

exceptional moments in his life. I remember him as caring, as one who cried—cried so often it was unnerving. He had a passion, a tenderness, a patience with God's people that I have never seen in any other man.

As I look back to those days in Antioch—and then in Jerusalem—it was a time that defined the very gospel, and I thank God that Paul forced himself into boldness. It was not like Paul to do these things. He denied himself to become that man for an hour. I know, for I have seen him crying, shaking, and utterly at a loss as to how to help the churches when they faced various crises. I have seen Paul uncertain . . . even when he was certain.

I will now tell you the full story of what happened at that banquet. Not the rumors you may have heard, but the truth.

But first I must say that the brothers who had spent the day with Paul heaved a sigh of relief as they watched him storm out of that room and head toward the banquet hall. Until that moment all hearts were filled with dread. Everyone feared that Barnabas and Paul would agree with Blastinius. As Paul left the room that day, some smiled, some wept. But every man there recognized that he had found his champion of *grace alone!*

CHAPTER 24

The farewell banquet was held in a large rented room, the largest room in all Antioch. There were nearly two thousand people in the hall at the time of that unforgettable moment!

Paul opened the door and walked in after the others had already entered the banquet hall. He swept the room with his eyes, and what he saw caused his blood to boil. He saw Blastinius and his party of circumcised believers sitting in the back of the hall, separated from the Gentiles. And he saw Barnabas standing in the center of the room.

It was a moment of high drama. Those who were present that afternoon have told me they could actually see Barnabas struggling within himself. Every eye in that quiet room was focused on him, watching as he tried to decide whether to sit with his Gentile brothers or with the party of the circumcision. For an instant it seemed that he would sit with the Gentiles. But then he yielded. He turned toward the back of the room and sat down next to . . . Peter. Peter, who had *already* yielded to an old weakness: acceptance . . . pressure to conform . . . fear of what others thought of him. Peter was sitting next to Blastinius!

As Barnabas sat down, a voice shattered the silence, not unlike a lightning bolt. Paul began to move across the room and headed straight for Peter. As he went he spoke, thundering every word as he moved.

Not a soul in that room could believe his eyes or ears. "Simon Peter," Paul cried as he moved slowly, so agonizingly slowly, toward the back of the hall. Peter turned, startled, with a look no man could interpret.

"Simon Peter, how is it . . . ?" Paul was not yet halfway across the room, moving slowly, deliberately. Everyone wished he would somehow get there faster. Paul was driving the entire room into this confrontation by his slow pace, his thundering voice, and his calm demeanor. He intended for every believer in that room to hear his every word, and he intended that no one would forget the slightest detail.

Barnabas bowed his head. Blastinius was livid. Peter was as calm as Paul, his face still inscrutable. Every eye was trained on Paul.

"Simon Peter, how is it that you have eaten with the Gentiles each day until today . . . until this group of Pharisees from Jerusalem arrived? Until they came, you ate with the *Gentiles*. You ate with men who are *uncircumcised*. You ate with men who are *unclean*. Now you, and all the Hebrews in this assembly, refuse to eat with them. You won't sit with men who are uncircumcised. You won't sit with the unclean. Are you better than those who are uncircumcised?"

Paul's eyes narrowed on Barnabas. "Are *you*, Barnabas?"

He turned back to Peter. "I have a question for you, Peter. You are a Jew, are you not?" (Paul still had not reached Peter's table; the tension was excruciating.) "Yes, you are a Jew, but you don't live like a Jew. Peter, *you* live like a Gentile!

"And why do you live like a Gentile? I'll tell you why, Peter. It's because you failed in your attempt to live like a good Hebrew! You *know* you failed. You *never* succeeded at living up to the demands of the Jewish laws. You *cannot* live the way a

Hebrew is supposed to live." Paul paused but never took his eyes off Peter. Then he added, "And neither can Barnabas."

The tension in the room was unbelievable. Some began to weep. Paul was finally getting close to the table of the circumcised, but he never lowered his voice, and he never lost his unbelievable calm. At this point he looked directly at a man he had not seen in a score of years. "And, Blastinius, neither . . . can . . . you!"

Paul had now closed the distance between himself and Peter, and he finished with his finger in Peter's face. He continued to speak in a voice loud enough so everyone in that great hall could hear him: "Since you, a Jew by birth, have discarded the Jewish laws and are living like a Gentile, why are you trying to make these Gentiles obey the Jewish laws you abandoned? You and I are Jews by birth, not 'sinners' like the Gentiles. And yet we Jewish Christians know that we become right with God not by doing what the law commands but by faith in Jesus Christ. So we have believed in Christ Jesus, that we might be accepted by God because of our faith in Christ—and not because we have obeyed the law. For no one will ever be saved by obeying the law."

When he had finished with Peter, Paul did the most wonderful of things. This man, burning with fury, turned around and met the eyes of every one of his beloved Gentile friends. A quiet smile made its way across his face. (He was so calm it hurt!) There was a nod of his head. Somehow, in that simple gesture and with accompanying tears, Paul was able to say to a thousand Gentiles, "It's all right; you are inferior to no one. All is well."

Still calm and still moving slowly and deliberately, Paul walked over to a table full of scruffy-looking Gentiles and sat down. Then in a voice that could probably have been heard all the way to Jerusalem, he said, "May I please have some *pork?*"

There was an instant of stunned silence, broken by a spontaneous peal of laughter. Some of the Gentiles even began to applaud.

Blastinius was consumed with unmitigated hate. He had been outdone, and Paul had won back the hearts of the Gentiles. And adding insult to injury, Paul had brought an end to the whole battle in an ovation of laughter. Blastinius could have known no greater demeaning. It was in that moment of blind rage that Blastinius declared war on Paul. It was a war that lasted throughout both of their lives.

It became proverbial to describe that afternoon in these words: "The last time the church of Jesus Christ had seen such drama was at the Resurrection!"

The next morning Peter left Antioch. The party of Blastinius vanished, but no one knew that they actually remained in the city almost a full week. Then they emerged to confront Paul.

Long before Peter arrived back home in Jerusalem, word of what had happened in Antioch reached the ears of the ecclesia in Jerusalem. There were rumors everywhere. And those rumors persist to this day. But I can now tell you exactly what Jerusalem's reaction was. I know, for I was in Jerusalem at the time! Listen carefully to my words.

CHAPTER   2 5

Paul rebuked *Peter!*"

The rumor spread like wildfire through the ecclesia in Jerusalem. When I first heard it, I was speechless. "Paul rebuked Peter? Surely not! No one rebukes Peter."

I simply could not believe it. How could the greatest apostle be rebuked by a former persecutor of the church of Jesus Christ—a man about whom there was already much doubt and suspicion? Had that man dared to rebuke the very person whom the Lord Jesus had chosen as leader of the Twelve?

"Paul rebuked Peter!" That sentence was followed by the astounding statement that "he did it in the presence of two thousand people!"

I cannot tell you how shocked I was, how shocked we all were. I felt sure of one thing. This man Paul had no place in the work of God! At that moment, I would not have followed Paul across the street. I doubt I would have allowed him through the door of my room. And I doubt the church in Jerusalem would have received him as a brother in Christ. Nor was there any thought in our minds that he would ever again be received by the churches in Judea. Paul had committed the unpardonable insult. No one could have convinced me that the apostles would soon shake Paul's hand, embrace him, give him the kiss of

Christian love, and send him out to preach the gospel of Jesus Christ to the heathen nations.

Even an archangel would not have persuaded me that I, of all people, would one day be Paul's companion and fellow worker in raising up assemblies of *Gentiles.*

Paul was finished, and I knew it. Such were the feelings of every believer in Jerusalem. *Until Peter arrived!* And until a letter from the ecclesia in Antioch also arrived.

That is when we learned what Blastinius had done when he went to Antioch with the letter from James. Suddenly we realized there might be two sides to this story.

When the believers in Antioch wrote to the ecclesia in Jerusalem, they did not know where Blastinius was. Further, his Pharisee friends, having returned to Jerusalem, refused to say where he had gone. (In fact, it would be months before any of us heard where Blastinius had gone and what he had done.) All of us began to wonder if there was more to this story than we had first assumed.

Follow me now as I tell you the whole story, for some aspects of the situation have never before been fully revealed.

⚭

After Peter left Antioch, there was a withering confrontation between Blastinius and Paul. By now Barnabas was back at Paul's side. A Pharisee from Tarsus and a Levite from Cyprus confronted a company of Pharisees and scribes from Jerusalem for an entire day! No one gave ground. It was a furious confrontation.

Immediately after that battle of words, Blastinius disappeared entirely. The next day the brothers in Antioch came together to discuss what to do. They prayed and talked for two days and nights without food. The brothers in the room who were Jews repented of their vacillations, Barnabas among them. (It was on that day, I believe, that Barnabas became his own man, for when he later came to Jerusalem, he was a lion among men. I know. I was there, and I watched him.)

The decision the brothers finally reached was simplicity itself. "We were living in peace and joy. Then these men came from Jerusalem and created a great crisis among us. The problem came from Jerusalem, so the problem should be addressed in Jerusalem and hopefully *solved* in Jerusalem."

The brothers in Antioch then wrote a letter to the elders in Jerusalem. They also addressed that letter to the entire church in Jerusalem. It was a short letter. At least the message was short, but the letter was signed or "marked" by every brother in Antioch!

"Men claiming to be from James," the letter said, "have disturbed the faith in Antioch. We are sending a delegation of men from the ecclesia in Antioch. We request that you who are leaders in the church in Jerusalem receive these men as brothers in Christ, and we ask you to give us instruction in these matters.

"The delegation includes our beloved brother Barnabas, and Paul, and a Gentile named Titus. All are messengers from the ecclesia that gathers here in Antioch."

One of the brothers was chosen to take this letter to Jerusalem by horse and with all speed. The brother actually arrived in Jerusalem only shortly after Peter did and *before* the circumcision party had arrived. When the messenger from Antioch arrived in Jerusalem, he found Peter and gave him the letter.

Peter's words, when he took the letter from the horseman, were brief. "I will deliver this letter personally to the apostles. Tell your delegates that they will be warmly received, and this matter will be thoroughly addressed."

When the rider returned to Antioch, another letter was immediately written by the brothers in Antioch and again sent by horseman to Jerusalem. The letter simply estimated when the apostles in Jerusalem might expect the brothers from Antioch to arrive.

Where was Blastinius? His Pharisee friends had returned to

Jerusalem. (They were busy reinventing the events in Antioch.) But where was Blastinius? None of his company would say, and it was many months before we learned the awful truth.

On his last day in Antioch, after his confrontation with Paul, Blastinius made an audacious decision. The story is nearly beyond belief. None of us, not even Paul, could have guessed what Blastinius would do. But his action showed the measure of his hatred for Paul, his obsession with the law of Moses, and his commitment to destroy Paul's ministry—no matter where Paul went and no matter when he went there.

When Blastinius ended his debate with Paul, he realized how formidable was this enemy he had sworn to destroy. (Paul also realized he had met a man every bit his peer.) One man stood immovable for law, rules, demands, good deeds, and Christ. The other stood simply for Christ.

Blastinius Drachrachma left that meeting that day and went to *Galatia!*

In his mind, Blastinius could see those four churches in Galatia. He could see them planted by two upstarts who did not understand the Jewish gospel. He shuddered to think that the men in those churches were uncircumcised. So Blastinius concluded they were assemblies not of Christians but of heathens. But even more infuriating was the idea that those churches even existed. He was sure those people did not have divine life. Therefore, he concluded, someone must go to Galatia and circumcise those people or—failing that—destroy the churches!

On the day after the debate, most of the Pharisees departed for Jerusalem. Everyone assumed that all of them were returning to Jerusalem, but that's not what happened.

Blastinius told his followers what he had decided to do. Even they were shocked. But these were his instructions: "Leave Antioch. Return to Jerusalem. See to it that the true gospel is victorious in Jerusalem. Tell everyone that Paul has profaned the Lord by insulting Peter and by denying the law of

Moses. Tell *everyone*, believers and nonbelievers. Let the city hear. Let all men learn to despise Paul. But I will not go with you. As you depart south for Jerusalem, I will travel north to Cilicia and then on to Galatia."

"You are going to *Galatia?*" his friends asked incredulously. "You're going to visit those four heathen churches? Why?"

His answer was clear, and it was final. "I will take Zebulun, the scribe, with me. I will go to Galatia, and I will follow Paul's footsteps and visit all four cities. I will see to it that those who assemble in those four places hear what this false apostle has done. I will carry James's letter of introduction; and I will carry a knife and, with it, the *true* gospel. Those Gentile heathens in those spurious churches will hear the true gospel from me. If any refuse my words, I will do all in my power to destroy them. But I think that need not be. Paul is wrong, and I am right. Truth will triumph. Now do not let Paul know I have gone to his Gentiles. I will need time, but I have no doubt that Galatia will come into the fold."

Then Blastinius, in the presence of all those Pharisees, took a blood-chilling oath. It was a vow worthy of the dagger men who, some years later, vowed to take Paul's life. "Before almighty God, whom I serve with all my heart, I commit my life henceforth to seeing that Paul's message is destroyed. I swear to the God I love that I will go anywhere and everywhere that Paul plants Gentile churches. I will follow him to the ends of this earth until the day God strikes him dead. Wherever I follow him, I will tell every Gentile assembly he starts . . . I will tell them the truth of God. I will bring them to Abraham and Moses, or I will do all in my power to destroy them. Thus shall it be as long as I live."

His friends muttered a few prayers and quickly departed. Zebulun, only slightly less zealous for the law and every bit as learned in it, began preparations for the long, arduous journey to Galatia.

I remind you, Paul knew nothing of this journey to Galatia. And it was a year later that he learned of the oath Blastinius had taken. Even now it seems unbelievable that Paul, Barnabas, and Titus were on their way to Jerusalem at the very time that Blastinius was on his way to Derbe, Lystra, Iconium, and Antioch of Pisidia. At the very time Paul was in Jerusalem meeting with the apostles and standing for the grace of Jesus Christ alone, Blastinius was in Derbe proclaiming his gospel of Christ and circumcision.

◈

Paul, Barnabas, and Titus arrived in Jerusalem late one evening. Since the elders were anticipating their arrival, they had already planned a closed meeting for the next morning. James invited me to attend this meeting along with the apostles, James himself, the Jerusalem elders, and a number of other brothers. We would meet with the brothers from Antioch, and we would stay at it, no matter how long it took, until this conflict was resolved. Has there ever been, or will there ever again be, so momentous a gathering? I think not. (Incidentally, I was both surprised and honored to be invited to this gathering. Why I was invited, I am still not sure.)

The room was small and crowded. When I entered, I was taken aback by some of the faces in the room. Many Pharisees who insisted on being there were present. (Several of them had been in Antioch, and it turned out that they were the real problem.) They were told they could sit in, even speak, but not be part of the deliberation nor the final decisions to be made in this matter. I noticed immediately that Blastinius was not present, but I thought nothing of *why* he was not there. Certainly I never dreamed he was in Galatia.

There was more tension in the room—and more nervous men—than I had ever expected. I pitied the elders from the church in Jerusalem, for elders had only recently been appointed.

Paul, Barnabas, and Titus (the brother of Luke) chose to sit in a corner. I had seen Paul only once before—several years after his conversion. He had preached the gospel during that brief visit to Jerusalem, but many years had elapsed, and he was certainly better known for his zealous persecution of the believers prior to his conversion. It had been a long time since I had seen Barnabas. And seeing a Greek—Titus—in the midst of so many Jews was very odd. Titus seemed to enjoy the whole affair. He was a young man who loved his Lord, as I came to discover, and he was almost carefree. He *knew* he was a believer.

But most of us were staring at Paul and Peter. Would there be another explosion between them? Who would be revealed as the more godly in word and attitude? To our surprise, it turned out that nothing at all happened between them. It was as though the incident in Antioch had never happened!

Peter began the meeting. He started with a request that none of us discuss these meetings with anyone. We all knew this would be difficult, for every believer in Jerusalem wanted to know what was going on. Nonetheless, it is only today, in my old age, that I can tell you what happened in that room during those next few days.

For one entire day we listened to Barnabas tell his story of leaving Jerusalem—at Peter's request—and traveling to Antioch, and of the first four years in the life of the ecclesia there.

I enjoyed hearing Barnabas's story. He and I had been added to the Lord on the same day—the day of Pentecost. We had been close friends (along with Philip, Stephen, and Agabus) during those first seven years. We had sat together day after day in Solomon's Colonnade, listening to the Twelve as they recounted their years of living with the Lord in Galilee.

Barnabas, by the way, had written down everything he could. His young nephew Mark sat beside him and later made a copy of Barnabas's notes. Years later Mark sat with Peter for days, writing down everything Peter told him about the Lord. Then Mark wrote a complete account about the Lord's life. But you are, of course, familiar with that story.

The Barnabas I now listened to was not the Barnabas I had grown up with years before in Solomon's Colonnade. This man held his own convictions; he was his own man. In the past his adoration of Peter and of the Twelve had been limitless. Now he was ready to stand up to these men, if necessary, in order to broaden *their* understanding of the gospel. And he did this out of his deep love for the Gentiles. His one taste of returning to the bondage of the law, the day he sat down with Blastinius, had set him free indeed.

As Barnabas spoke to us, he gave Paul great credit for the work in Antioch and, even more, for the work in Galatia. He also made a point of quoting from messages Paul had spoken. I began to see Paul in a wholly different light. So did most of the men in the room, except, of course, the Pharisees who had been in Antioch.

What happened after that meeting became a riotously humorous story we all love to tell. It was late when Barnabas finished, and we agreed to meet again early the next morning. Barnabas, Paul, and Titus returned to the place they were staying. A few minutes later, Barnabas rushed outside. This was followed by a yell and some scuffling, and Barnabas came back into the room dragging a Pharisee by the scruff of the neck! "He was peeping into our room!" Barnabas said angrily. "What were you doing at our window?"

For twenty minutes the culprit came up with one excuse after another, none plausible.

"You will tell us the truth, or you will stand before James," Barnabas said with finality.

The man paled. "We wanted to find out if Titus had been circumcised," he finally admitted.

"You what?" exclaimed Barnabas.

Titus fell back on his mat in disbelief. Barnabas was trying his best not to laugh, but it was a losing battle. Paul burst out laughing. Titus remained wide eyed and speechless.

"Spying on a man to see if he is circumcised!" said Barnabas, throwing up his hands in dismay.

"The ends of the law!" roared Paul, still laughing.

By now Titus was indignant. "Who sent you?"

"No one."

"You said *we.*"

At that point the Pharisee jumped up and darted out into the night. Titus ran after him, but it was too dark to try to pursue him. So Titus called out after him, "I am as blameless as Abraham was on the day God declared him to be righteous, and I have just as much skin as he had!"

Barnabas and Paul, standing in the middle of the street, were in convulsions. Titus, still indignant, managed a grin. The incident became part of Gentile Christian lore.

Word of what happened soon reached every ear in Jerusalem. Titus told the story several times the next morning. As he began retelling the story to the apostles, they were undone. But by the time Titus finished, they were in tears, they had laughed so hard. Even James had to stifle a smile. There were apologies from all over the room, and the troublemakers were very much on the defensive.

As the business of the day began, Paul was asked to speak. He had already made Barnabas and Titus terribly curious, for he had come into the room with a small bundle in his hand.

As Paul stood to speak, I must say I was still very skeptical. Who was this man? Almost everyone in the room shared my skepticism of this Jew from a Greek city. Despite his brief visit years before, he was almost completely unknown to us except that the Pharisees hated him. Beyond that, only rumors. But before Paul could begin, Barnabas spoke up. "My brother Paul is as fine a man as has ever walked among us. Most of what you know of him is secondhand. Hear him. Hear him well, for he is your brother."

Paul said, "You know all too well of my early career as a zealous Pharisee. I did everything I could to destroy the church. I went from house to house, dragging out both men and women to throw them into jail. Some of you were whipped or beaten as a result of my zeal, and I apologize to you.

"I even received authorization to go to Damascus and find the followers of the Way and bring them in chains to Jerusalem to be punished. But as I was on the road, nearing Damascus, a very bright light from heaven suddenly shone around me. I fell to the ground and heard a voice saying to me, 'Saul, Saul, why are you persecuting me?'

"'Who are you, sir?' I asked. And he replied, 'I am Jesus of Nazareth, the one you are persecuting.' The people with me saw the light but didn't hear the voice.

"I said, 'What shall I do, Lord?' And the Lord told me, 'Get up and go into Damascus, and there you will be told all that you are to do.'

"I was blinded by the intense light and had to be led into Damascus by my companions. A man named Ananias lived there. He was a godly man in his devotion to the law, and he was well thought of by all the Jews of Damascus. He came to me and stood beside me and said, 'Brother Saul, receive your sight.' And that very hour I could see him!

"Then he told me, 'The God of our ancestors has chosen you to know his will and to see the Righteous One and hear him speak. You are to take his message everywhere, telling the whole world what you have seen and heard. And now, why delay? Get up and be baptized, and have your sins washed away, calling on the name of the Lord.'"

We had all heard the story before, but this time it came

from Paul himself. We were enthralled. Truly this man had met the Lord.

Paul continued his narrative. "I immediately began preaching in Damascus, and many of our own people there became convinced that Jesus is the Messiah. But then the Jewish leaders decided to kill me—so I escaped by being let down in a large basket through an opening in the city wall!

"Instead of returning to Jerusalem immediately, I went to Arabia, where the Lord put me through a time of refining solitude. From Arabia I returned to Damascus, and finally I came back here to Jerusalem three years after my conversion. I spent fifteen wonderful days here with Peter and James." He nodded in their direction. "They were a bit cautious at first, but they spoke to me for days on end about our Lord's life and ministry. Then I traveled through Syria and returned to my hometown of Tarsus in Cilicia.

"A few years later I visited Jerusalem again. Some of you will remember that visit, even though it was quite short. You were understandably afraid of me, but Barnabas vouched for me that I was indeed a brother in the Lord. But that visit was cut short when my life was threatened by some of the Greek-speaking Jews, so I returned to Tarsus.

"A few years later, when Peter sent Barnabas to Antioch, Barnabas traveled to Tarsus and asked me to help him in Antioch. I was pleased to do so, and we spent a wonderful year in ministry together there. I participated in the daily life of the church and worked each day in the marketplace as a worker of leather and mender of tents.

"I did nothing there except what all brothers do. Other things I did came by way of invitation from the brothers. All during this time I sat at the feet of Barnabas, learning from him the things he learned from *you.*" There were nods of approval around the room.

"It was during that period that the ecclesia in Antioch asked

Barnabas and me to bring their gift of grain to you here in Jerusalem. But that was during the time of the persecution under Herod Agrippa. Most of you were in hiding, so we never had a chance to meet with the entire ecclesia here.

"This is my fourth visit," he said. Then he added, "I trust there will be no persecution this time . . . at least not of you." The irony brought smiles.

"That is all, except to emphasize that I have always earned my bread with the work of my hands."

Barnabas interrupted. "Over and again Paul asked me to tell him everything about Pentecost and about the Jerusalem church and what it was like for the believers when he persecuted them. He wanted to understand everything from the viewpoint of the ecclesia. I told him all I could of the gospel, including everything you men had told me about your years with Jesus. I also read to Paul everything I had written while listening to you in Solomon's Colonnade. As any good student, he repeated back to me everything I said to him. My brothers, Paul did to me what Silas, Stephen, Philip, and I did to you. He pelted me with questions." The apostles, remembering back to the eager young Barnabas, nodded and smiled.

Our view of Paul was shifting. Only the Pharisees remained entrenched.

Some sisters appeared and served us a sumptuous meal. As I ate, I could not help but look around the room at the men present. I wondered if Peter had fully forgiven Paul by now, and I had no indication of what James was thinking.

When the meeting began again, Titus told of his conversion and growth in Christ. Several men had not been in the morning meeting but had heard of Titus's adventure the night before. They asked if Titus would tell the story again. I breathed easier as I watched Peter again roar with laughter.

That evening Paul began to tell us about the two years he and Barnabas had spent in Galatia. We cringed as he mentioned that he had received thirty-nine lashes on Cyprus. The story of the shipwreck was breathtaking, and the tale of their harrowing experiences on the road from Perga to Pisidia shocked us all. We cringed again when he told how they had both been beaten with rods in Antioch of Pisidia.

As Paul told the stories, he always placed Barnabas at the center. Barnabas, in turn, would have none of it. He would insert his own recollection of the events and place Paul in the forefront. As the evening progressed, it became one story told by two men. We sat in silence, except for our sobs and tears.

Twelve men, all of whom had experienced persecution, knew they had *never* gone through such pain as Paul and Barnabas now described. They were impressed!

Barnabas's recounting of Paul's being stoned moved us deeply, but then one of the Pharisees questioned whether all these stories were true. For the first time ever, I saw Barnabas flash rage. He ripped off his shirt and asked between clenched teeth, "Do you see this back? It is nothing compared to Paul's. I won't honor you by showing you Paul's scars. But look at his face; there are scars enough there!"

"None of us has paid so dearly," said John quietly.

"We believe you, brother Paul," I choked.

"I, too, believe," said Peter. "But there are some here, like Thomas used to be, who only believe what they see, Paul."

Paul, his eyes filled with tears, begged, "Please, Peter. I'd rather not."

"Yes, Paul," whispered Peter.

It was the loudest silence I have ever heard. Finally, Paul turned around and, acquiescing to Peter's request, pulled off his shirt.

None of us will forget that moment. Peter sobbed. So did we all, except the Pharisees. Paul quickly donned his shirt again, sat down, and buried his head in his hands.

Barnabas broke the awkward silence. "He was whipped more

than once, shipwrecked in the cold waters of the Mediterranean for a night and a day, and beaten with rods." He paused. "Near Pisidia, naked and frozen, he almost died." He paused again. "Then he was *stoned*. Yet I have never heard him complain. He should have been bitter or angry or at least had the good sense to go home. But no, none of that. Instead, he was always anxious to preach Jesus Christ. Further, Paul preaches about his Lord with a depth and an energy I have never heard in any other man."

Barnabas's face was like flint, his eyes burning like fire. Glaring at the scribes and Pharisees, he sat down.

Paul asked for a final word. It was then that he opened the mysterious little bag he had with him. He pulled out a scroll. It was part of a Hebrew Scripture. Where had this man managed to lay hands on sacred Scripture? And how had he managed to get permission to bring it into such a place as this? For Scriptures were found *only* in synagogues, where they were locked in strong wooden and copper boxes. As he opened the scroll, a torch was passed to his side. Paul struggled to read in the dim light. "Perhaps someone with younger eyes . . ."

Titus was on his feet in an instant. "Oh, it's Hebrew," he said—and then sat back down, blushing. Everyone chuckled. Most of the people in the room were past forty, an age beyond which most men's eyes were no longer strong enough to read. To everyone's surprise, a scribe stepped forward, took the scroll, and began to read.

> "The Lord spoke to Abram in a vision and said to him, 'Do not be afraid, Abram, for I will protect you, and your reward will be great.'
>
> "But Abram replied, 'O Sovereign Lord, what good are all your blessings when I don't even have a son? Since I don't have a son, Eliezer of Damascus, a servant in my household, will inherit all my wealth. You have given me no children, so one of my servants will have to be my heir.'

"Then the Lord said to him, 'No, your servant will not be your heir, for you will have a son of your own to inherit everything I am giving you.' Then the Lord brought Abram outside beneath the night sky and told him, 'Look up into the heavens and count the stars if you can. Your descendants will be like that—too many to count!' And Abram believed the Lord, and the Lord declared him righteous because of his faith."

The story was familiar to all. When the scribe finished, Paul began to speak quietly. "Abraham was a son of Babylon. Today, by our standards, he would have been called a Gentile—at least up to that moment when he was declared righteous. He was a Gentile and was *still* uncircumcised and had *no* knowledge of the law of Moses (for Moses would not appear for another four hundred years)—yet God declared him righteous!"

It was a telling point. But a Pharisee, seeing how the meeting was shifting toward Barnabas and Paul, blurted out, "Yes, but God took Abraham by the hair of his head and carried him four hundred years into the future and caused him to sit at the feet of Moses."

An awkward silence filled the room. Peter coughed, trying hard to cover a laugh. John didn't even try. He laughed out loud. After a moment the room burst into laughter. I believe it was in that moment that the brothers began to see the simplicity of the problem and the ridiculousness of too much learning (or perhaps too much religion).

It was the ever-stern James who called the meeting to an end. As we departed, we all knew that the next day would decide everything. James had said that the issues would be discussed by all. After that, a decision.

Although this all happened so many years ago, I would still prefer not to recall the next meeting.

CHAPTER 26

We did not eat a bite of food that next day. The party of the circumcised attacked Paul, attacked Barnabas, attacked Antioch, and was especially vitriolic about the four churches in Galatia.

Barnabas and Paul answered every word. Often Peter or John had to intervene to keep order. So much Scripture was quoted that our heads spun. But no one sitting in that meeting could disagree with this fact: Paul of Tarsus had a grasp of Jesus Christ and the gospel that was as well-founded as that of any man in the room. No more did I question that fact!

Barnabas and Paul had changed our hearts, our minds, our prejudice—and had reduced the rumors to nothing. Truly they were lions among men.

The debate finally ended. My stomach was in a knot. I dreaded what was to come. Two men in that room held the key to the future of the gospel. I had no idea where either stood. The other eleven, yes, but Peter and James had revealed nothing of their foundational beliefs in this matter.

Peter broke the tension. His words amazed me: "Brothers, you all know that God chose me from among you some time ago to preach to the Gentiles so that they could hear the Good News and believe. God, who knows people's hearts, confirmed that he accepts Gentiles by giving them the Holy Spirit, just as he gave him to us. He made no distinction between us and them, for he also cleansed their hearts through faith. Why are you now questioning God's way by burdening the Gentile believers with a yoke that neither we nor our ancestors were able to bear? We believe that we are all saved the same way, by the special favor of the Lord Jesus."

Think back to Antioch, where Paul rebuked Peter at the banquet. Peter had a weakness of crumbling under the pressure of men. But he had a greater strength in that he could break with his mistakes, confess his weakness, repent, and move on to a boldness that none of the rest of us had. Now, in the crucible of debate between the Pharisees on one hand and Paul and Barnabas on the other hand, Peter had quoted Paul! He used the same argument Paul had hurled at him in the banquet room in Antioch. Truly the Lord had worked in the soul and spirit of that man during those days.

When Peter finished, I thought the issue was settled. I had forgotten about James—the man who had been carried in Mary's womb and grown up in the same house with Jesus, a man who looked so much like Jesus it was uncanny.

If you have never met James, it might be hard for you to understand his influence in Jerusalem. To many, the brother of Jesus ranked higher than the Twelve. Such is the power of kinship in our culture, and James was kin to *Jesus!* And when we looked at James, his features conveyed the face of our Lord! Never underestimate that factor. Further, James was a man of legendary piety. He spent his life in prayer, including in his prayer life the odd habit of never placing a rug beneath his knees. Some surmised it was James's way of repenting for having come late to believe in his half brother as the Messiah.

My heart stopped when James cleared his throat. I prayed. Oh, how I prayed. "Dear Lord, let this people yield to grace." That prayer changed my life, for my own life had chains I could not see. Such is the case of most Hebrew zealots who are for Christ *and* for the laws and the scrolls.

Surely you have heard what James said. His mind had leaped over a hundred issues and had come all the way down to the practical matters of the moment. It took the rest of us a minute to catch up with James. No questions. No issues. Just a practical way of settling this issue.

"Brothers," he said, "listen to me. Peter has told you about the time God first visited the Gentiles to take from them a people for himself. And this conversion of Gentiles agrees with what the prophets predicted. For instance, it is written:

> *'Afterward I will return,*
> > *and I will restore the fallen kingdom of David.*
> *From the ruins I will rebuild it,*
> > *and I will restore it,*
> *so that the rest of humanity might find the Lord,*
> > *including the Gentiles—*
> > *all those I have called to be mine.*
> *This is what the Lord says,*
> > *he who made these things known long ago.'*

"And so my judgment is that we should stop troubling the Gentiles who turn to God, except that we should write to them and tell them to abstain from eating meat sacrificed to idols, from sexual immorality, and from consuming blood or eating the meat of strangled animals. For these laws of Moses have been preached in Jewish synagogues in every city on every Sabbath for many generations."

Paul wept openly. His tears moved Barnabas to cry. Several of the apostles joined them. Paul had a *dozen* new friends.

Someone got up, went over, and hugged Paul. Everyone joined in. That is, everyone except the party of the circumcised, who stalked out as soon as James finished speaking.

As we walked back to our rooms that night, about a score of

us locked arms and began to sing as we walked. Paul couldn't contain his euphoria. And in the coming days I must have heard him break out in shouts of joy dozens of times. Even on the way back to Antioch he would suddenly break out in praises to the Lord.

Word of the decision spread through Jerusalem that very night. Most of the church had heard before dawn. The next day the entire ecclesia gathered together and asked Paul if he would speak. I believe he considered it the highest honor he had ever received. At last Paul of Tarsus had been fully accepted by the other apostles and the thousands of holy ones in Jerusalem.

Paul and Barnabas wanted to return to Antioch immediately. Before they left, however, the elders decided that two others from Jerusalem should go with them to Antioch to verify the events that had taken place in Jerusalem and to attest to the authenticity of the letter they carried.

Judas Barsabbas was selected to be one such messenger. To my surprise, I was also selected. To this day I don't know how this choice was made. It was one of the highest honors of my life. On the other hand, looking back, I see that my going to Antioch set off a series of events that almost cost me my life—several times!

∞

The letter James had suggested was written and then signed by all who had been in the council meeting. Even I was allowed to sign the letter. I understand the letter still exists and is treasured by the church in Antioch. There are over twenty names on it, including Peter's illegible scrawl!

When all the signatures had been affixed to the scroll, John placed it in a small leather satchel and handed it to me. On the scroll was written this message:

This letter is from the apostles and elders, your brothers in Jerusalem. It is written to the Gentile believers in Antioch, Syria, and Cilicia. Greetings!

We understand that some men from here have troubled you and upset you with their teaching, but they had no such instructions from us. So it seemed good to us, having unanimously agreed on our decision, to send you these official representatives, along with our beloved Barnabas and Paul, who have risked their lives for the sake of our Lord Jesus Christ. So we are sending Judas and Silas to tell you what we have decided concerning your question.

For it seemed good to the Holy Spirit and to us to lay no greater burden on you than these requirements: You must abstain from eating food offered to idols, from consuming blood or eating the meat of strangled animals, and from sexual immorality. If you do this, you will do well. Farewell.

CHAPTER 27

The next day we departed for a nation and a city I had never seen. With me were Paul, Barnabas, Titus, and Judas Barsabbas. Barnabas had invited his nephew John Mark to return with him to Antioch, so he also traveled with us. Despite Paul's disappointment with Mark several years earlier, he had no objection to Mark's joining us. I must confess, we were talking, laughing, and praising all the way to Syria.

As we made our way north, we stopped at every assembly along our route. In every town the entire assembly came together and listened to us speak of the momentous news from Jerusalem. And in all those places the Hebrew believers gladly welcomed the news that Gentiles had been added to the members of the elect and had been received as part of Christ's body.

During that trip, a close friendship began growing between Titus and Mark. They always walked at the back of the company, talking as only young men do. Mark spent hours telling Titus the story of the life of Jesus. Titus kept insisting that Mark write some of this down so that he, Titus, could make a copy for himself. Mark felt that his uncle should do this, but Barnabas protested, "It should be done by an eyewitness to the Lord's life." Soon we were all discussing just who that person should be. Peter's name was never mentioned, of course, because he was illiterate. (We did not know at that time how well Mark could write, nor did we know that Peter would be so willing to work with him.) I have always felt that the time Mark and Titus spent together on that journey marked the first time Mark had thought of writing a simple story of Jesus' life. Today, so many years later, Mark's book and Paul's letter to the Galatians are the two scrolls most circulated among the assemblies.

As I write these words, I think of the irony of our situation. There we were, en route to a Gentile church, our purpose being to confirm Gentiles' freedom in Christ. But at the very same time, Blastinius Drachrachma was in Galatia moving among the Gentile assemblies in Derbe, Lystra, Iconium, and Pisidia, taking *away* their freedom, enslaving them to the law, and driving them to rules and legalism.

As we entered Antioch, just what was Blastinius doing up in Galatia? What was he saying in the gatherings of the four assemblies? We must know the answer to these questions if we are to understand why Paul wrote so audacious a letter to those four ecclesias. If you understand what Blastinius did, you will understand the letter to the Galatians. Understand what Blastinius did, and you will understand why Paul acted as he did. Today that letter of Paul's is at the center of the controversy that still envelops assemblies all across the Roman Empire. It is time to shine a light on those events.

Perhaps if I unfold this story, it may help bring an end to the controversy surrounding that letter.

CHAPTER 28

Derbe. That was the first place where Blastinius was received. Would the foundation Paul had laid two years earlier survive the presence of Blastinius? If you had known Blastinius, you would have been certain it would not and that Blastinius would win. This man had made a dangerous journey of hundreds of miles for the sole purpose of winning the hearts of these churches—or destroying them.

I, Silas, have made the same journey Blastinius made. It takes great passion of purpose to make that long, hard trek. Long days, hot days, sleeping in fields, staying in rat-infested inns, rain, cold, heat, mountains. Blastinius was driven by a passion most of us will never know, a passion driven by religion and pure *hate*. That man, it turned out, would sacrifice and suffer as much as Paul did. All that to preach his gospel—his "good news" of obedience to the law. He preached it as fervently as Paul did the gospel of Christ.

A born leader, Blastinius was as cunning and magnetic as any man ever born. A formidable opponent for anyone, by any measure. This is the man God placed in Paul's life, there to remain for as long as Paul lived.

Arriving in Derbe, Blastinius and Zebulun presented themselves as messengers from the church in Jerusalem and from

James. They had a letter from James to prove it! The believers in Galatia were ecstatic. "At last, visitors from Jerusalem! Just think, we can hear from someone in our sister church first-hand." Such were the thoughts of these innocent believers.

Blastinius was given great honor by everyone in the ecclesia. When he spoke in the meetings, they clung to his every word. Those dear believers were simplicity itself, and Blastinius was at his best.

"Someone from Jerusalem has cared enough to come to visit us. And, oh, the things he says . . . and what a holy man." In a matter of hours Blastinius was being treated with as much honor as Paul. No one knew there was a circumcision knife waiting in his luggage.

Blastinius had presented his letter from James and Jerusalem with great flourish, explaining that James was the brother of the Lord Jesus. "And James asked me to bring you greetings from him and from the entire church in Jerusalem!" The assembly was like clay in Blastinius's hands.

Paul had raised a people in purity and great innocence. Blastinius, who would never have been so foolish, was taking full advantage of Paul's wonderful weakness. Blastinius told the believers in Derbe exactly what he knew they would want to hear. He told them of the Lord's life and of the ecclesia in Jerusalem. He exalted James and Peter in every way and constantly referred to Jerusalem as the mother church. He strongly emphasized the persecution Paul had caused, vividly recalling Paul's cruelty. He never mentioned Paul's conversion, but he told of his own conversion in glowing terms, clearly leaving the impression that he was one of the most respected and trusted leaders in all the churches.

Derbe was taken in. Soon they became troubled by this good man's reluctance to speak well of Paul. Once more he was able to convey, without words, the impression that he was far too godly a man to speak ill of someone else. This only heightened everyone's curiosity and led to silent doubts about Paul. Silent doubts—the strongest of all doubts! Blastinius knew exactly what he was doing, and what he was doing was working. His gospel was winning a church.

I have often said, "No man ever had such an opponent as did Paul in this man Blastinius." The subtle insinuations continued. The Lord's people became more and more curious and doubtful. Always seemingly reluctant to speak evil of another, Blastinius feigned pain each time he added a new disparaging word about Paul. Step-by-step, Blastinius exalted himself and demeaned Paul. Such is the power of religion, as religion appeals to the religious nature of all men.

Finally, the ever-pious Blastinius reluctantly and painfully relented and told them his truth about Paul. "Paul, you see, is a coward," he confided. The people were stunned. "He wasn't man enough to tell you *all* of the gospel. He was afraid that you might turn from following *him*. If you had heard all of the gospel of Christ, you might not have had the courage to respond to the gospel. But I trust you. I believe you have such courage."

Blastinius had won. He began telling the believers in Derbe the entire history of the Hebrews, including the stories of Moses and the six hundred laws of Moses. And circumcision, which he said "is the rest of the gospel, the part the coward Paul left out, the painful part." Blastinius was making sure that Paul was totally destroyed in their eyes.

"Before I invite you to respond to all of the gospel, you must understand one more thing. As much as it pains me to do so, I must tell you what Paul did while he was among you and what kind of man he really is. And if you insist on knowing, I'll tell you what he did in Antioch. Then you will also know why James sent me here. Paul carries no respect in the churches. How could the assemblies respect him after what he did? Terrible."

"What did he do?" everyone wanted to know.

"You haven't heard? I saw what he did with my very own eyes."

"What?"

Grimacing and appearing to struggle within himself, Blastinius finally revealed the terrible truth. "Paul rebuked Peter!"

The holy ones in Derbe were not exactly sure what that meant, but they appeared to be shocked nonetheless! Blastinius did an excellent job of explaining. "Jesus appointed Peter as leader of the Twelve. He is revered by all. He represents the true gospel of Jesus. Paul does not believe that gospel. Paul is arrogant, and he has placed his opinion above Peter's. In Antioch I watched him dare to rebuke Peter, and he did it in the presence of two thousand people. Peter was sitting beside *me* at the time."

Blastinius let it sink in that *Peter* had been sitting beside him. "Then he rebuked *me!*"

The room fell silent. The holy ones were aghast. "For this reason, the Jerusalem church will never have anything to do with Paul again. He is finished among the *real* churches."

The holy ones in Derbe sat in disillusioned silence. A sense of hopelessness fell on everyone.

"Let me illustrate. When Paul came here to you, did he have a letter with him from Jerusalem?" Everyone looked around in confusion. Most were not even familiar with what a letter was, having never received or sent one.

"No," replied one of the Greek merchants.

"He had *no* letter?" said a mortified Blastinius. (The way Blastinius said it, you would have thought he'd taken lessons from the serpent in the Garden.) Everyone was appalled. Some began to weep.

I ask you, could a church survive this?

"One last thing. Did Paul call himself an *apostle?*"

Several nodded yes, deciding to hear more dark words about Paul, the man who had fooled them.

"Only the church in Jerusalem can send out apostles," said Blastinius pompously. "He, therefore, is not an apostle. Paul, I fear, has lied to you."

The destruction was complete. Knowing he had won, Blastinius launched into a grand explanation of the centrality of Jerusalem, going all the way back to David and the Jebusites. Over and again he emphasized "mother Jerusalem." Then he reemphasized Peter's prominence. "Without the approval of Peter and the approval of the Jerusalem church, you really have *nothing.*" Derbe had a new and wonderful hero, come to set them free from error.

Blastinius then explained, in anger, that the only reason Paul had come to Galatia was that he had no respect anywhere else. More weeping followed, while others shook their heads in sad silence. "This man never allowed himself to be taught. Never has he submitted himself for instruction to Jerusalem nor to the Twelve. Why has he never come to Jerusalem? Why would he not submit to the mother church?

"Now this plague named Paul has come here. My presence here is to give you the completed gospel—something that man pleaser dared not do!" Blastinius paused. "Perhaps Paul fears being persecuted," said Blastinius in a fading voice. This left his listeners confused, however. Paul did not seem to fear persecution. Obviously Blastinius did not know Paul very well, they thought.

Nonetheless, Blastinius pressed on. "You must be sons of Abraham to be right in God's eyes. Moses gave us over six hundred laws, ordinances, commands, and regulations to obey. It is only when we obey these laws that God finds us pleasing in his sight. And not until then!"

"Six hundred and how many?" asked Gaius.

"Approximately 633, depending on who is counting," replied Blastinius.

Gaius leaned forward. "What of Barnabas?" he countered.

"He lived in Jerusalem some thirteen years, did he not? He said he did. Did Barnabas lie to us?"

For an instant, Blastinius was caught off guard. Everyone sensed his momentary uncertainty. But Blastinius skirted the question, implying that Paul must have misled Barnabas.

This raised more uncertainty, however, for trying to imagine Barnabas being misled by Paul, or anyone, was difficult for these Galatians to do.

Undaunted, Blastinius continued toward his goal, the one he had traveled hundreds of miles to accomplish. He finally said it. "To be a son of Abraham you must be circumcised. It is a *painful* experience, one that will hurt for days, perhaps even giving you an infection. That is what Paul feared to tell you lest you refuse to follow him. Yet you must be circumcised, as was Abraham, to have right standing in God's eyes."

"What's circumcision?" someone asked.

Blastinius blinked in disbelief at their ignorance and then explained the procedure. He continued, "There is a difference between a Greek and a Jew. The difference is one of cleanness and uncleanness. Uncircumcised, a Greek is *unclean*. Circumcised *and* obeying God's law—as given by Moses—you *can* become clean and acceptable to God."

"What must we do?" asked a brother intensely.

"On the Sabbath we will observe the rite of circumcision. Those who wish to be counted as sons of Abraham and counted right with God can meet with me beside the stream north of the city, there to be circumcised."

A few more questions were asked. Blastinius then repeated a memorized prayer and dismissed the meeting—a meeting he was in total charge of. The people, disturbed and defeated, went to their homes that night.

Gaius remained to ask a few more questions. A handful of brothers who were still in the room tarried to listen. The exchange between the two men was intense. Blastinius took the position of a patient father to a renegade son. Gaius did not yield to the lesser role.

That night, back in his room, Gaius made a bold decision. There was not a single soul in the ecclesia in Derbe who was of Jewish heritage. Gaius needed to talk with someone who was. Asking two other brothers to go with him, Gaius left Derbe *that night* to visit Lystra. As the three men walked those twenty miles, they reviewed their doubts and formulated questions. Just before dawn they arrived at the home of Eunice.

All day they plied Eunice with questions. Lois and Timothy (who was now twenty-one) listened in silence. Eunice helped the three men understand many of the stories in the Hebrew Scripture, but she could give them no final conclusion as to what to do.

"We have only three days before the Sabbath," Gaius observed in exasperation. He looked up. Timothy was on his feet. "Yes?" said Gaius, trying to discover what Timothy was doing.

"Call all the brothers together. Now. All of them." That is all Timothy said.

So it was done. All the men in the assembly met together in Eunice's home. Excitedly and with a mustard seed of hope, Gaius rehearsed with all the Lystra brothers everything that had happened in Derbe. An hour or more of discussion followed, but still no one was certain what they should do.

Once more Timothy stood. "All the brothers who can must leave here immediately and go to Derbe." There was finality in his voice. Everyone sensed total and instant agreement. His words were the ones they needed to hear.

"When we arrive, what shall we do?"

"We will tell all the brothers in Derbe not to do this thing. Not yet. *Wait.*" Timothy paused. "We shall say to them, if we can be deceived by such men as Barnabas and Paul, then we can just as surely be deceived by Blastinius."

Silence thundered. That is all Timothy said. Four sentences in one night. But those sentences changed everything!

Another brother stood. "Yes. As many as can, let us leave here and go to Derbe, *now*. If we hurry, we can arrive before nightfall."

The next evening the brothers in Derbe found themselves packed into a small room with the brothers from Lystra. No one really knew what to do or whom to side with. That is, no one but Timothy. "Much harm may come to the two assemblies if some of us act on the word of this man. No harm will come in waiting." Words so simple, yet so true. A decision was made.

That very night the brothers from Derbe, accompanied by twenty-one-year-old Timothy from Lystra, went to the inn where Blastinius was staying, to tell him of their decision. "We will wait."

Blastinius fought hard to contain his rage and maintain his facade of piety. When he began his act, and it was a very compelling act, Timothy was not drawn in. When Blastinius began to treat young Timothy with disdain, Timothy grew in age. When he argued with Timothy, the young Greek held his own. When Blastinius commented on Timothy's ignorance, Timothy flashed an intelligence no one knew he had. And when Blastinius ordered Timothy to obey him, Timothy was outright defiant!

Blastinius was first outraged by so stubborn a youth, but then he regained his composure and gave a priestly sounding conclusion to the evening. "Of course, what I have brought to you, these are all new words to you. The God of Abraham and Moses will be with you and show you these things. I will leave you to your decision. I will return in a month to know of your decision—Paul or Moses."

The Derbe brothers breathed a sigh of relief. No ugly confrontation or debate would have to be experienced *in* the church. And men from both churches kept glancing over at

Timothy, wondering where this young man had suddenly emerged from.

But even as the Galatian believers were relaxing, Blastinius and Zebulun had other plans for other places. By daybreak they were on their way to Iconium. There would be no Timothy to stop them there.

Had Blastinius failed? No, Blastinius had done his work: Two churches were in confusion, and many brothers had lost all confidence in Paul. For Blastinius, that was victory enough. And as Blastinius had predicted, there was no one like Timothy to stop him in either Iconium or Pisidia. What follows is a sad story indeed.

CHAPTER 29

Blastinius deceived Iconium the way he had deceived Derbe. Following the same pattern, he undermined Paul's teaching by preaching his gospel of faith in Christ plus circumcision plus the Hebrew laws. The only difference was that he introduced the gospel of circumcision so that those who believed him would be circumcised the very next day. Many believed, and many were circumcised, but doubts about this man and his gospel did surface.

Blastinius had a way of feeding such dissension. He truly did not care if it destroyed the assembly. What saved the hour?

Timothy! That young man walked all the way to Iconium from Lystra. Upon his arrival he called the brothers together and, even more boldly than in Derbe, spoke to them in unequivocal words. The brothers asked him to address the entire gathering, for the church was divided in its sentiments.

Timothy asked for love above opinions and for patience. "Wait, and place care above divisive doctrine."

When Timothy left Iconium, the church was on its knees before the Lord, seeking his direction. It was an uncertain situation. And Blastinius? He was well on his way to Antioch of Pisidia. It was there that he had his greatest success.

Remember, no one in Jerusalem or in Antioch of Syria knew

what was happening in Galatia. Paul and Barnabas were home in Antioch basking in the joy of victory. Paul had no idea Blastinius was in Galatia, nor could he have imagined the depths of Blastinius's gift for deceiving those believers.

Now we must return to Antioch of Syria—and to the saddest part of our story.

CHAPTER 30

Our group of six—Paul, Barnabas, John Mark, Titus, Judas, and I—arrived back in Antioch late in the afternoon. Nowhere had I seen such a beautiful city, with such broad thoroughfares. Nor had I ever seen so many Gentiles and so few of my own people. The sounds, the accents, the features of the people, their ways and customs, even the smell of the city were all new to me. Yet I had the impression that Paul sighed with relief at being back in this heathen world.

Many have asked my first impression of the Antioch church. One word: *freedom*. Believers interrupted one another; there was laughter and spontaneous singing. Some of this I had seen, but never with so much liveliness. Also, their closeness and their *touching*—this was very un-Hebrew. When I inquired of this closeness, the blithe answer was, "We are kin."

Of course, everyone wanted to know how it had gone in Jerusalem. "Far better than anyone had hoped," was our reply.

It was my privilege to open the letter from James, Peter, and the other apostles before the entire assembly. Afterward everyone wanted to see Peter's signature, knowing he could not read or write. What Peter had written was no more than a meaningless scrawl.

"Peter is as unlettered as he claimed."

"Yes," I replied, "but Peter told me that he's determined to learn to read."

"Will he learn to write, also?"

"He's not sure. He says he may be too old to learn anything so difficult."

Paul and Barnabas told in great detail all that had transpired in Jerusalem. When it came to the part about Titus's being spied on, they let Titus tell the story himself, for by now he was able to tell it as no other could! Again and again the assembly laughed with glee. Then Judas and I bore witness that the letter and the signatures were authentic and that the story of what happened in Jerusalem, as each man told it, was true.

Everyone in the church grasped the gravity of the crisis and the miraculous outcome. Surely now—at last—Antioch was a sister church to Jerusalem and to the ecclesia in Judea. And Gentiles need not be circumcised.

Questions came in abundance. But what astounded me was how everyone interrupted each other, and no one seemed to mind. That was my first experience at being interrupted. And laughter was never far away. I also noticed that Paul and Barnabas, though respected, were not held in such awe as the Twelve were in Judea.

I was not long in Antioch before I began to notice a few chains and inhibitions of my own falling away. I had been warned it would happen! I also began to realize the vast implication of allowing the doors of salvation to be opened to heathen. The gospel and the church were losing their isolationism, their prejudices. Most of all, the faith was losing its Jewish culture. This had never happened before. In every city, in every province, in all the world where Jewish believers had gone, there was the Judaization of the faith. But now the gospel and the ecclesia were losing that singular, universal expression. The ecclesia would be different in every culture and province, strongly reflecting diverse cultures wherever it was planted. My heart rejoiced, though my mind was a bit reluctant.

For days it seemed that about the only thing I did was show the Jerusalem letter to curious brothers and sisters. Always it was the same. "Which one is Peter's signature?" Peter was a man still much loved and admired, especially by the Hebrews among them in Antioch.

Sometimes I wish I had returned to Jerusalem about that time, so as to be spared seeing what happened next because it pained us all so deeply.

You have heard of the conflict between Barnabas and Paul. I was there. The falling out began with a single statement. "Let's go to Galatia and see how the four assemblies are doing." Those were Paul's words. (Mind you, when Paul made that suggestion, he had no idea Blastinius was in Galatia laying waste the churches there.) "We can show them the letter from the apostles in Jerusalem. Of course, they will probably see no significance in the letter, since most have no idea what circumcision is."

Then came the rift. Barnabas proposed that they return to Cyprus first. He wanted to show the letter to the churches there, in hopes that the Cyprus churches might at last open themselves to the uncircumcised Gentiles. Paul did not like the idea.

"Ever since we left Jerusalem I have been thinking, *This changes everything on Cyprus,*" said Barnabas. "Now I can return to my island home, tell them what happened in Jerusalem, and show them this letter. And finally we can preach to the Gentiles on Cyprus and bring them into the gathering of the body of Christ." Paul was silent.

"Why not?" urged Barnabas.

"Will it really change anything?"

Barnabas was caught off guard. "Paul, we can proclaim Christ to the *Gentiles* on Cyprus!"

"But will it liberate the Jewish ecclesia? Or will they go on as they are?"

"You mean . . ."

"I mean the churches on Cyprus are bound in ways far beyond circumcision. We know that we Hebrews don't easily change. The Gentiles would be miserable going to a synagogue and performing all those rituals—stand now, sit now, listen now, go home now. We were called and sent to Gentiles, but not to Gentiles who would then be placed in a Jewish culture."

"They can change. They will," reasoned Barnabas.

So began the dispute. After much heated discussion Paul reluctantly agreed, but with the understanding that they would go *first* to Galatia and *then* to Cyprus. The matter seemed closed, though the agreement was fragile.

Then came the explosion. Barnabas insisted that Mark go with them. Paul would have none of it. The contention between the two men broke the bounds of civility. Both said things they regretted.

Paul made one point to Barnabas that I will never forget. "Barnabas, it is the sentiment of every believer to return to the place of his youth to proclaim the gospel to kin and old friends. I have that feeling toward Tarsus. But it is not a wise thing to give in to. In most cases, it is something to be denied."

Those were wise words, but the issue of Mark could not be circumvented. Finally, a decision was reached, but it was reached in heated anger and unguarded words. The two men decided to go to separate places—one to Cyprus, the other to Galatia and beyond.

I must say this to Barnabas's credit. He graciously let Paul carry the original Jerusalem letter with him. It proved to be a wise capitulation. Barnabas did not need the original. For Galatia, the original letter would prove to be crucial.

As you consider the breakup of this legendary friendship, remember that those two men had lived in peace with one another for four important years in Antioch. Further, they were as one man during those two years in Galatia. Then, returning home again, they continued working together. Beyond that, they were a wall of unity when they went to Jerusalem together.

Remember, too, that a more single-minded man than Paul never lived. He was a man beyond description, heedless of danger, pain, and inconvenience. I tell you truthfully, two years of raising up churches with Paul would test the ends of any man. I know, for I traveled with him on his second trip!

Barnabas made a copy of the Jerusalem letter, and a few days later he set sail for the land of his youth, his nephew at his side.

Barnabas did a marvelous work in Cyprus. No other man could have done what he accomplished there. But as Paul predicted, the older assemblies did not change. Barnabas made no headway there, not an inch. But then he went to the towns and villages where there were no assemblies and few Jews. Those new assemblies were vibrant and wholly Gentile.

I have heard it said that these two men never worked together again. This is not true. Years later Paul invited Barnabas to come to Greece to minister to the ecclesia in Corinth at a time when Paul needed all the quality help he could find. Barnabas agreed and sailed to Corinth from Cyprus to help out in the Corinthian situation. Peter, Apollos, and Barnabas all ministered in Corinth, but only Barnabas's presence turned out to be a help rather than a hindrance.

As Luke observed in his history, Barnabas was a good man, full of the Holy Spirit. I miss him sorely.

As for Mark, when he matured he became a man of stature. Years later, in Paul's old age, he and Mark became friends and coworkers once again.

Now I must tell you what happened when Paul found out Blastinius was in Galatia!

CHAPTER 31

Barnabas had hardly departed Antioch for Cyprus when a letter came to Paul from Galatia. It came the very morning Judas Barsabbas and I were making ready to return to Jerusalem. When Paul read the letter, he was livid. "Some Pharisee in Galatia is destroying God's assemblies there."

"Who is it?" we all asked.

"The letter doesn't say," responded a frustrated Paul. "Whoever he is, he is circumcising the Lord's Gentiles!"

Paul, enraged but still wise, made several unusual decisions. One was to write a letter to the four young ecclesias. My first big surprise came when Paul told me that he would postpone his trip to Galatia. "I will not leave until I know my letter has had time to reach all four of the Galatian churches. I will go to them only *after* they have received it."

Paul turned to the Antioch believers and said, "I will need a traveling companion. Who should go with me when I do leave?"

The answer was immediate and certain: "Silas should go with you to Galatia. He was the one who brought us the letter from Jerusalem; he is the one who read the letter to us; he was in the meeting with you in Jerusalem; therefore, Silas should be the one to go to Galatia to attest to the letter's authenticity."

I agreed reluctantly.

Now we come to Paul's controversial letter. It was a letter that, as I look back, may very well have led to Paul's death some fifteen years later.

The letter to the Galatians! Paul's best-known epistle. The one most copied and most read. Even to this day it is copied and circulated. It was written in Greek, but it has been translated into Aramaic for distribution in Judea. And of course it is widely circulated among the Gentiles everywhere.

As I tell you about Paul's writing of that letter, let me remind you that I, Silas, was in the room with Paul on the day he wrote it.

CHAPTER 32

A Pharisee up in Galatia visiting the churches," Paul moaned. "Who? Why? Silas, how shall I behave? How shall I deal with this?" Paul was full of questions and fears.

This is what Paul and I were finally able to piece together: Someone from Jerusalem had gone to Galatia. He visited every church and told them he had a letter from James. He told the assemblies that Paul was merely trying to gain their favor, and he called Paul a coward. He said that Paul was not trusted in the other churches, that he was not an apostle, and that he had not been sent out by the Twelve. The mother church, he said, would have nothing to do with Paul, and Paul avoided visiting it. Paul was afraid to preach the entire gospel. He held Jerusalem in contempt and was an outcast because he had openly rebuked Peter.

This man even had the Gentiles obeying all the Sabbath laws and watching the phases of the moon so they would know when to observe Jewish holidays. All this plus circumcision. Paul had neglected to tell them all this "gospel."

"I have been painted black on black, and God's people have been hurt," muttered Paul.

The final outrage for Paul was the statement "Antioch is

not authorized to send out apostles; only Jerusalem has that authority."

One thing was obvious: This genius at twisting truth had preached a gospel that men could be justified in God's eyes only by trusting in Christ *and* obeying all Moses' commands *and* being circumcised. Paul was devastated that the Gentiles had even heard such words. There was urgency in getting a letter written and delivered to Derbe, the nearest of the churches.

Paul consoled himself with one thought. The Pharisee in Galatia, whoever it was, was not up to date in his information. The circumcision issue had been settled. As to the man's having some important letter from James, Paul was furious. "He has a letter from James, has he? Well, I have a letter from James, too . . . signed not only by James but also by *all* the apostles."

Paul started several times to write to Galatia, then decided to wait until his anger completely abated. (A first draft was blistering; he threw it away and waited.)

In that time of waiting, Paul went before his Lord and surrendered his own will and all four churches to God. Then, still unsure about the state of his heart, he told the Lord he was willing to see all the churches be destroyed. "Whatever pleases you, Lord."

I have seen Paul do many selfless things, but one of the memories that I treasure most is seeing him surrender his will to the worst thing he could imagine: the destruction of the Galatian churches.

Paul finally felt sure that his anger was under control. He then asked me to spend the day with him. When I entered his room, I saw that an amanuensis was also present. He was one of the brothers in the Antioch ecclesia. Why an amanuensis? Why did Paul not pen his letter in his own hand?

There is a saying among those who cannot read:

Why learn to *read?*
By the time you are thirty-five
your eyes cannot see
what is written on the paper.
Why learn to *write?*
By the time you are forty
you cannot see the paper!

Paul was past forty-four, hence the amanuensis.

I sat down, and Paul began talking softly. We must have talked for hours. It was his way, at least that day, of preparing to write a letter. Paul and I also talked to the amanuensis so he might have some idea what was about to be written and why.

"Silas, it is not true that Jerusalem is our mother. Not the Jerusalem we see here on earth. Our Jerusalem is above. She is in realms unseen. Above. Invisible, in heavenly places. We have a Jerusalem, but not this one. Our Jerusalem is above.

"Sinai is not our mountain. Nor is our covenant the covenant God made with Moses. We have a mountain, but not Sinai. Abraham was an uncircumcised Babylonian when he was declared right with God. All the apostles agreed with that. Abraham lived four hundred years before Moses. They never met. *That* covenant, the one God made with Abraham, is the first covenant. It is spiritual, and that is the covenant that is *ours.*

"As to freedom, over half of all our brothers and sisters are slaves, and most of the others once were. Freedom invaded their lives when they believed that freedom is Christ himself. They changed. Today even slaves are free.

"If you do not begin with utter freedom from the law, if there is one iota of the law where you are not free, you live your whole Christian life in fear of that one rule. Yes, fearful. Fearful that God will not accept you if you fail at that one point. There can be no exception. If you are free of the law, then you are free to be the Lord's. *Only* then are you utterly free to be the Lord's. All law, Silas. All rules, Silas. All rightness, Silas. All."

"Isn't that dangerous?"

"Dangerous? Perhaps. But to present anything that could take you out of his grace . . . *that* is dangerous. A gospel that presents as a solution Christ plus one iota of law—that is far less than an uttermost solution. His solution is an uttermost solution. If it is Christ and the dot of an *i*, then Christ died in vain . . . for then his deliverance is not utter deliverance. My Lord's solution, my Lord's salvation, is *utter*. Silas, a freedom that is freedom from every possible prohibition does not cause a believer to sin. It is a freedom that sets the believer free to love him—with all the others in the assembly—to love him with all their hearts."

I swallowed hard. "Do you tell believers this, Paul?"

"I do, everywhere I go. That is what causes his people to love him. 'Such an amazing Lord,' they say. 'How could I not love so amazing a Lord as that!' They are astounded at such a Lord."

Paul's words frightened me. But one day I met the believers who had heard his audacious and seemingly dangerous gospel. They did love the Lord, like no believers I had ever seen or heard of. They were as devout in life as any Jew. I have to say I never saw their equal in love and purity of life. Yet, churchwide, these truly free saints were not even aware they had either freedom or purity. There was a Christ-centeredness about them I had never seen. Christ was their point of reference in all things. *Uprightness* was not what was going on in Galatia. *Love of Christ* was what I experienced in Galatia.

Gentiles without laws but with Christ were as righteous in life as any man living in the obedience and unending bondage that goes with trying to keep an endless list of rules.

Paul changed the subject. For a long time he talked about the flesh and the spirit and the Cross—and all that had been destroyed by that Cross. To hear that man talk of what had *already* been crucified shook me to my foundation. More of my chains fell off. Nonetheless, I shuddered to think what that letter was going to say.

There was a depth, an otherworldliness about Paul's gospel that was unique from all the rest of us. That man really had seen the unseen and touched the invisible. His gospel was one that saw through God's eyes, not human eyes. For Paul to sit there and tell me how God saw me left me speechless. No wonder Paul so often called the believers *holy* ones. He saw the saints as God sees us.

So went the day. Suddenly Paul stopped. He was ready. And now, that infamous letter!

CHAPTER 33

Paul took a deep breath and then began dictating the incredible letter. It was not a letter to individuals, mind you. Never read it that way. That letter is to a church. (Well, to *four* churches.) Not to you. Not to me. He wrote that letter to a group of people in an assembly—an assembly of uncircumcised ex-heathens. He wrote it to a community.

I never moved or spoke during the whole time Paul dictated the letter; rather, I sat transfixed. He never stopped or corrected or changed. He knew every word he wanted to say. He had struggled with an earlier draft, but this time the man was inspired!

As Paul neared the end of the letter, he took the pen from the amanuensis, squinted his eyes, and wrote a sentence of his own in large letters, so large that even a man over fifty could read it.

When he seemed to have finished, I asked, "Are you done?" I'm sure I sounded doubtful.

"Yes," Paul answered. "Why? Did I leave something out?"

"You sure did, Paul. You left out the main point!"

"What?"

"Paul, you never mentioned that you had a letter from

James and the apostles approving your teaching. How could you forget to mention it?!"

Paul smiled. "I didn't forget."

I stammered on. "And you never told them you would soon be visiting them. Not a word. Here we are packed to leave, and they don't know we are coming. How could you forget that?"

"I didn't forget," he said, chuckling.

"What?!"

"It would be most unwise to mention that we are coming to visit them."

"Unwise?" I protested. "Paul, someone has ruthlessly attacked you. He's telling the Galatians that you rebuked Peter and that Peter no longer has anything to do with you. But right here in my hand is a letter commending you—with Peter's signature on it. And James's! Paul, in the name of wisdom, tell them so! Tell them that all the apostles have agreed that Gentiles don't have to be circumcised. And tell them we are coming to visit."

Paul's eyes twinkled. "Silas, no matter what this letter to Galatia contains, some will reject it. Some will not believe a word of it. A man from the party of the circumcised has done much damage. He has made real converts in Galatia. Some believe his lies and believe them very fervently. A letter from me, no matter what it says, will be rejected by them. A good general always holds back some of his best soldiers in reserve. My letter will bring almost everyone back to Christ—but not all. It won't matter if I tell them of the approval I have from the twelve apostles or of the letter from Jerusalem. But when word of my arrival passes from one church to another, some who doubted will begin to doubt their doubts. When word reaches them that I have a letter from Peter—and when *you* stand up in the meeting and tell everyone the story of what happened in Jerusalem and read the very letter signed by James and Peter—*that* will change everything."

What could I say? This lion among men had an insight into men's ways that most of us will never have. His was a master stroke.

The letter, four copies in all, left Antioch the next day. The brothers had hired a horseman to deliver it to Derbe. The brothers in Derbe were to see that it was sent on to the other churches as fast as their means could afford.

The next day Paul and I departed Antioch on foot. Strange, but my brother Paul, as was sometimes his nature, became depressed beyond all consolation.

How often I heard him whisper, "Only four months. I was with each of them only four months. Has my gospel held? What might I have said to them if I had known such a crisis was coming? What warning should I have given? Or should I have warned them not at all?

"Will there be Galatian churches when we get there? Please, God, will I be welcome? It was, after all, a hard letter. Perhaps too hard. Have I lost them all? Perhaps I built with straw. Please, Lord, I hope I built with unburnable gold."

Hearing Paul speak that way filled my own heart with anxiety. And if I had known it was Blastinius who had gone to Galatia, I would have known for certain that all was hopeless. Was the church of Jesus Christ still in Galatia? Was Paul still welcome? These questions now burned in both our hearts.

"I was there for only four months, Silas!" he wailed. "My gospel may not be confirmed by other men as being the true gospel, but if they do not approve it, still it is *his* gospel. I proclaim Christ. And *Christ is the gospel.*"

We soon fell to talking about Paul's letter. "Paul," I said, "are you aware that you mentioned the gathering in Jerusalem with James and the apostles, then *later* in the letter you wrote about confronting Peter? You mentioned those two events in reverse order. You confronted Peter in Antioch; *then* you went to Jerusalem. Won't this confuse some?"

"I think not. Who will read the letter anyway? Just the Gentiles in Galatia. I'll explain it to them if they are confused. After all, this letter isn't going anywhere but four places. I doubt it will ever be read by anyone else. In a few months no one will even remember I wrote it."

How wrong we were. It seems everyone on earth has read that letter. And there has been much confusion as to which event took place first. Luke sought to clarify the point in his account of the church planters. I hope these memoirs will finally clear this point.

As Paul and I walked along, I saw a window into Paul's humanity. He was truly afraid he had *already* lost all four of the churches. "I only hope we are not too late. Silas, we may find no churches in Galatia. Or we may find there are churches, but they may have forever rejected me." He repeated the anxieties over and again with many tears. It was, in truth, a sad and burdened man who drew near to Derbe.

CHAPTER 34

In the ninth year of the reign of the emperor Claudius, Paul of Tarsus and I, Silas, passed into the area of Asia Minor called Galatia. Our fears grew with every step. The final two days we hardly uttered a word. Outside the Derbe gates we paused. We laid everything at the feet of our Lord. Then, holding our breath, we stepped into the marketplace. We were consumed with the fear of the unknown, and we certainly were not prepared for what happened.

A shout rang out. Someone came running toward us, yelling as he came. The brother grabbed Paul and began swinging him around. Paul, in turn, was trying hard to grasp the moment, but he was smiling hopefully. Because of this brother's incessant noise, others in the marketplace began looking at us. Another brother appeared. They both wrapped themselves around Paul. One of the brothers was Gaius.

"Paul! How are you?!"

"I will tell you as soon as you allow me to catch my breath! Has the letter arrived?"

"Oh, yes, yes. It was wonderful!"

"*What?*"

"It was wonderful."

"It was *what?*" Paul asked again, for the first answer did not

fit. It was written to save a church, true, but "wonderful" didn't
fit. Paul had simply failed to count on what love could do. (He
also knew nothing of Timothy's awesome intervention.)

"We have read it three or four times in the meetings. We
didn't know you were such a good writer."

Paul was a blend of confusion and surprise. "You . . . you
liked it?"

"Yes, and do we have a story to tell you! Something wonderful has happened here."

"*What?*" asked a still-stunned Paul.

"You see, when Blastinius finally left, one of the brothers . . ."

"Blastinius! Do you mean Blastinius Drachrachma? Is he the
one who came here?" Paul's face turned ashen. My heart fell.

"Yes, *old Blasphemius* is what we call him now!"

Paul's legs about gave way. "Where is he?"

"I don't know."

"You don't know!"

"We don't care. Anyway, after Blastinius left here, Timothy
came from Lystra and began to help us. Oh, what a brother!"

"Where, in heaven's name, is Blastinius? How are the
churches? Timothy? Timothy who?"

Both Derbe brothers fell silent. "You don't know Timothy?"

"Eunice's son?"

"Yes, he's a man now." There was a sense of pride in Gaius's
voice.

"What did he do?"

"He put Lystra and Derbe back on the path to Jesus Christ,
that's what he did. And Iconium, too. Hallelujah!"

For a moment Paul began to wander off. He could not deal
with so much good news so quickly. Turning back to Gaius,
Paul asked again, "Everyone is all right?"

"Yes!"

Paul allowed himself to relax a little. He whispered quietly,

"Praise the Lord!" Then, still unable to grasp it all, he asked, "Are you sure?"

"Yes, Paul. Everything here is wonderful. And what a letter! I hope old Blasphemius reads it."

"What of Lystra?"

"Fine."

"Iconium?"

"We are not entirely sure—but hopeful."

"Antioch of Pisidia?"

Gaius shook his head. "We don't know. In the beginning they fell completely under Blastinius's spell. Since your letter was delivered, we have heard nothing."

Paul breathed hard. Still, he did not miss the point. Two churches had survived Blastinius. Plus, they had survived Paul's stinging letter.

Within an hour, more than half of God's people were in Gaius's home, hugging Paul and me furiously. That night we all met for hours. In fact, we stayed up all night. I read the Jerusalem letter to them. Frankly, no one seemed to be greatly impressed. There was only a lot of laughter because Paul had finally managed to have a letter recommending him. It was clear that the Derbe crisis was over and nearly forgotten.

After a few hours' sleep, Paul and I set out for Lystra, accompanied by several exuberant brothers.

The Lystra assembly was as strong as Derbe, perhaps stronger. Everyone was bursting with pride over Timothy. And with good reason.

When Timothy stepped forward to greet us, Paul eyed the young man as though he were meeting him for the first time. We spent the night in Eunice's home. Again we got little sleep. So it went for several days. Paul asked Timothy question after question, all day and on into the night. Brothers and sisters huddled around, just to listen and to glow. Later they got involved, regaling us with stories of the last few months, laughing uproariously as they went along.

Somewhere in all this, Paul discovered that Timothy had also traveled to Iconium. "You have been to Iconium? When?"

"Yes, several times. They keep on asking me to return. They have had many questions."

"Since my letter?"

"Oh no, *before* your letter. I suppose the letter has arrived there by now, but they were doing well before your letter."

Paul slowly shook his head as he watched the way Timothy handled himself. "You have changed."

"He just blossomed one day," declared Eunice.

Paul kept staring at the young man. "How old are you? Twenty now?"

Timothy nodded. "Twenty-one."

"Can you read?"

"Of course. Eunice saw to that."

"Do you know anything about the situation in Antioch of Pisidia?"

Timothy grew sober. "I have no idea. Only that I am told Blastinius made great progress there, that some were circumcised, and that there has been much dissension."

Paul looked at Eunice. "May I speak with you privately?" Eunice and Paul conferred in whispers for a moment. Then Paul came back and said to Timothy, "Tomorrow, Silas and I leave for Iconium. Will you come with us? It will be for several weeks only."

Timothy looked at Eunice. Eunice was radiant. "Surely!"

Timothy studied Paul's face. "And from Iconium where will you go?"

"To Pisidia."

"And from there?"

"Somewhere that the name of Jesus is not known. But I do not know where."

"I want to go with you!"

"What?"

"Not just to Iconium. I want to go with you for the rest of your journey."

I was not sure I was hearing what I heard. Paul looked at me, then at Eunice. "He is called, Paul," she said quietly.

"Are you?"

Timothy's answer was brazen. "As much as you, Paul."

Paul stared at Timothy in silence. "Then I have no choice. Nor do you, Timothy!"

Timothy broke into a broad grin and hugged Paul.

"There are hardships, you know," Paul cautioned.

"I know. Then both of us have said yes?"

"It would seem so."

The four of us talked until dawn.

❧

Paul later called the ecclesia together and separated Timothy to the ministry to which he had been called. Both soberly and joyfully, all the holy ones laid hands on him. Everyone wept, and no one as much as Timothy, though Eunice came close! Paul's charge and words of admonition to Timothy would have unnerved an archangel. He set a high standard for Timothy and, in so doing, for all the other Gentile workers who have followed. I have never seen an ordination for ministry that compared with Timothy's. And because no Gentiles had ever seen such a moment, they were in awe. My clearest recollection is the presence of the Holy Spirit.

At the close of the meeting, Paul said, "Now Timothy must be circumcised." Paul was great at paradoxes, but never as great as at that moment.

We were dumbfounded. Four churches had been in total confusion over this issue, and here was the most furious opponent of circumcision saying that someone had to be circumcised!

"For heaven's name, why?" Gaius blurted. And had he not spoken, I would have!

Timothy answered. His words were quick and wise and irrefutable. "Paul and I have spoken about this previously. Perhaps you do not know this, Gaius, but by Jewish tradition, the child of a mixed marriage cannot claim to be Jewish unless his mother is Jewish. So I am technically Jewish, but my culture is Greek, and you all know me as a Greek. My father was a Greek. I think as a Greek, and I have been schooled as a Greek. But I have learned from my grandmother the ways of God as thoroughly as any Jewish boy on this earth. If I choose this day to remain wholly Greek, I will be able to proclaim Christ only to the Greeks. But if I am circumcised, I will become wholly Jewish, and then I can proclaim Christ to both Jews and Greeks."

I shook my head. "When does the amazement end?" I wondered.

"In Christ there is no such thing as a Jew or a Greek," Timothy continued. "I know that. But Hebrews do *not* know that. Therefore, I will try to find common ground with everyone so that I can win them to Christ."

Timothy smiled, then added, "I learned those words from a Jew who grew up in a Greek city named Tarsus."

"You see?" Paul said to the rest of us. "I have been undone. Dare I speak against my own words?" He fell back against the wall in a gesture of surrender.

"Tell me, young man," I asked Timothy, "were you this hard on Blastinius?"

"Harder. Much harder," responded Lois, her ancient eyes brimming with tears.

❦

As we departed Lystra, I said to Paul, "You are a strange one, brother. Four churches have had no outside help since you left them two years ago, and now you take from them one of the only men among them who can read, write, preach, and lead."

"If you leave a church to Christ, his body, the Lord's people, will find ways to minister to itself. Timothy is not needed here. We have no priest. The church builds itself in the Lord."

Would to God others believed this. That day I marveled at this whole Gentile world of Galatia, where everything was so different from other places. "Such a man; such a people," I often caught myself saying.

Having walked for a few minutes, I stopped and looked back toward Lystra. *Who knows when Paul will return here?* I thought. *So little help, so strong a church, yet so untutored and poor a people. With all that, you survived Blastinius! No, beloved bride of Christ, you bested him!*

We arrived in Iconium in the middle of the night, for Paul was still an outlaw in that city.

In Iconium, as in Lystra and Derbe, we found that Paul's letter had been received well. Everyone spoke highly of Timothy and the help he had brought to them in their darkest hour. "Perhaps he's not a match for Blastinius, but he was certainly a strength to us in a deep night," one observed.

The church gathered the next evening. Paul brought words of comfort. Once more I read the letter from Jerusalem, and again it did not seem to be of great importance to the listeners. Paul's acceptance of them was all they seemed to want or need. The words of comfort we brought seemed to end the entire matter. I will always love the people in that assembly. They passed through much but came out a wiser, more mature people. And despite it all, they never lost their innocence.

I was also reminded that the Iconium church was even then being persecuted by the people of that city. Paul was still an outlaw, so our meetings with the ecclesia were clandestine. But you would never have known it had you not been told. Those dear people had an indomitable spirit.

"Antioch of Pisidia?" Paul asked publicly in the meeting. "Has anyone heard from Pisidia?"

No one knew anything except that Paul's letter had arrived there and that the believers in Pisidia did know Paul was coming. Paul's anxiety grew. That man suffered great travail for the assemblies. With everything weighing so heavily on him, he could hardly sleep.

A few days later Paul, Timothy, and I bade the Iconium assembly a reluctant good-bye and started out toward Pisidia. We had great foreboding, and it turned out to be a long and hard journey.

We finally arrived at an inn about ten miles short of Antioch of Pisidia. It was late afternoon. The innkeeper stared at Paul for a few moments, then asked, "Are you Paul of Tarsus?"

Paul hesitated. I froze. Just a few miles up the road Paul was a criminal. Paul took a deep breath. "I am." We knew that his identifying himself might very well mean we would be dashing out the door and into the woods at any moment.

The innkeeper smiled broadly. A strange reaction, we both thought. The innkeeper then walked outside and said something to a young boy. The boy looked up at us, smiled, then took off running. The innkeeper gave no clue as to what was happening, so we ate in haste and departed.

Outside we quickly devised a plan. All three of us would continue toward Antioch, but only Timothy and I would walk on the road. (Unlike Paul, we were not outlaws. We had never even been in this region.) Paul would make his way through the woods, alongside the road, staying out of sight but keeping us in view.

"When we get near Antioch," Paul said, "I will stop and remain hidden in the woods. You two go into the city and find some of the believers; that is, find a brother who is still willing to receive me. Bring him out of the city to me, and we will try to figure a way to smuggle me in—if there is reason enough for me to go in."

Paul paused. "I am assuming that the brothers and sisters still assemble and that some may welcome my presence. Find out if that is true and return to me."

Paul entered the woods as dusk was falling. We walked slowly and silently through the night until a road marker showed that we were only three miles from Antioch of Pisidia. We tensed when we saw two men sitting beside the road. Even though they looked innocent enough, we were apprehensive.

One of them called out to us. "Have you seen a man on the road tonight? Rather short, rather skinny. Somewhat old, gray headed, with a big forehead. He looks like a typical Jew. And he always carries a large leather satchel with him. Oh, and he's a little bow-legged."

Despite himself Timothy laughed. Fortunately Paul was far enough away that he did not hear this rather accurate description of himself.

I was at a loss as to how to answer the man's question. "Is he a robber?" asked Timothy.

"Oh no," came the reply. "He's my brother."

Timothy laughed. I cried. "Yes, he is behind us a ways, walking in the woods."

"Oh. Don't tell him that you saw us." With that, the two men began running toward the city.

In a moment Paul appeared. "What was all that noise about?"

We told him what had happened. He was as mystified as we were. But by this time we had lost some of our apprehension. After a few moments Paul went back into the woods, and we continued on our way. Shortly thereafter the night revealed to us the outline of the city. Then we began to hear strange sounds. We finally concluded there must be a garrison of Roman soldiers coming our way. We warned Paul to stay hidden.

Suddenly a torch was lit. Then another and another. The whole area before us burst into light. As the torches blazed forth, a voice burst into song. Christians! Scores of them. And, as usual with these Gentiles, they began to cheer, shout, and laugh all at the same time.

"Paul!" someone cried. The song changed. It was the entire assembly come out to greet us. Now they were singing a greeting. I began again to cry.

Paul stumbled out of the woods, and as he did, he was immediately engulfed. Poor Paul. He began to cry uncontrollably. I never saw him like that, before or after. He had completely gone to pieces.

We were about to become embarrassed for Paul when he suddenly dropped to his knees. Everyone knelt with him. After several moments of sobbing, Paul began to pray. His words were not fully coherent, but that prayer was one of the most beautiful outpourings of thanksgiving I will ever be privileged to hear. Others followed with simple prayers such as I had grown accustomed to hearing from these ex-heathens. Soon we were all crying.

Oh, these beautiful Gentiles! We sang and then sang some more. Then several brothers, raising their voices for all to hear, began to tell Paul of all that had happened to them since the arrival of Blastinius. It was Paul's letter, and that letter alone, that had convinced *everyone* as to who Paul really was and where the truth of the gospel lay.

"When it came down to it," said one of the brothers, "we all decided that we really preferred not to give up our freedom in Christ."

Paul's face, red and swollen, was aglow. Every word was balm to his heart.

"Let all this be reckoned to the account of the Holy Spirit and an indwelling Lord. *He* has saved his people, and no other," Timothy cried.

Right there, in the depths of the night, with torches providing light, we all sat in the middle of the Augustan Road and had a glorious meeting. There were so many tears, so many stories of God's grace, so much of the presence of God. Everyone had a story to tell. It was the best meeting I have ever been in.

And always there was the raucous laughter of the Gentiles.

Can you believe it? There in the dead of night, the sisters began bringing out food. We had a banquet right there in the middle of a Roman road.

While sitting there on the stone highway, I looked down at the small satchel that was hanging from a strap around my neck. I thought, *A letter from Jerusalem, signed by all the great leaders of Judea.* Then I murmured, "Well, dear letter, we all thought you were so important, but it turns out that you have been of no value whatsoever on this entire trip!"

Paul's letter alone had been sufficient. God had cared for his people through the life of a man named Paul. That man built with things that cannot be burned. When the fire fell, as fall it always must, imperishable things did not burn.

"Paul," I muttered to myself, "you did build with gold. Your works have been tested, and the gold has emerged from the furnace glowing with glory."

A little later a brother came to my side with a torch. "We heard you have a letter. Please read it."

I tried to read the letter, but I, too, was past thirty-five and found it difficult to read by torchlight. Timothy came to my side. What a beautiful sight. In the darkest part of night, torches everywhere, faces aglow with life and tears, Timothy took the letter and began to read. I can never forget that sight nor the sound of Timothy's voice.

There were no cheers. The Jerusalem letter was simply verification of what the Holy Spirit had already said to every heart. It was but a curious appendage to a dramatic series of events that had served to establish Christ and his wonderful grace deep in the life of the church.

Blastinius, we need more such visits from you, I thought. *Please come back. You were of great help to the gospel and to the building of the church.*

We arrived in Antioch of Pisidia at dawn and remained there for over a week.

∞∞

What happened next? We bade Pisidia good-bye. And yes—Paul, Timothy, and I eventually traveled to Greece. And yes—I would find out in Greece what a beating felt like, what a birch rod felt like, what a prison felt like, and what an earthquake felt like.

But now I close, for I have accomplished my goal: to tell you what really happened in Galatia.

You have met Paul as I knew him. You have seen God's pattern for the raising up of the ecclesia. This is how a church is supposed to be planted. An insane process, is it not? Yet it has God's fingerprints all over it!

You have also witnessed in this story the never-ending drama of what all of us must discover, that God is pleased with us—apart from our doing things to please him.

This is my prayer for you who read this story: that you will open the Galatian scroll—now so widely circulated—and read it again. And I trust that you will now understand what brought that letter into being. And understand what that letter is saying to all of God's people who hear the gospel as it was meant to be known. And never forget, the letter is to *churches*, to a *community* of believers.

May you discover freedom, and may chains fall off and never fetter you again. May you come to cherish that wonderful book of freedom, and, like the Galatians, may you be free indeed—with freedom that is Christ, for he is the freest of all.

Greet the holy ones—holy by no striving of their own.

May the abounding grace and even more abounding love of the Lord Jesus Christ be with you.

Amen!

EPILOGUE

When I first took up my pen to write this saga, I told you that Timothy was in hiding, that he was sick and at the point of death, not expected to live. By God's intervening mercy, Timothy has come back to us from the edge of death. I understand he is weak but growing stronger. Titus is alive! He has returned to us after a harrowing brush with death.

I have written to both Timothy and Titus, telling them of this diary. I have explained that I will write no more beyond this point in the awesome story. Nonetheless, I have urged both men to consider taking up the story from where I am leaving off. Timothy responded that he was still far too ill to think of such things. (Do not think of Timothy as still young. He is not. The events I recorded on these pages took place long ago.)

Titus responded by saying that he is reluctant to do so. But he did add: "Silas, if the diary you have written is well received by the Lord's people, I might consider continuing the story of that magnificent journey beyond the place where you have left off, for there is much to tell."

There certainly is!

Paul's Letter to the
GALATIANS

This letter is from Paul, an apostle. I was not appointed by any group or by human authority. My call is from Jesus Christ himself and from God the Father, who raised Jesus from the dead.

All the brothers and sisters here join me in sending greetings to the churches of Galatia.

May grace and peace be yours from God our Father and from the Lord Jesus Christ. He died for our sins, just as God our Father planned, in order to rescue us from this evil world in which we live. That is why all glory belongs to God through all the ages of eternity. Amen.

I am shocked that you are turning away so soon from God, who in his love and mercy called you to share the eternal life he gives through Christ. You are already following a different way that pretends to be the Good News but is not the Good News at all. You are being fooled by those who twist and change the truth concerning Christ.

Let God's curse fall on anyone, including myself, who preaches any other message than the one we told you about.

Even if an angel comes from heaven and preaches any other message, let him be forever cursed. I will say it again: If anyone preaches any other gospel than the one you welcomed, let God's curse fall upon that person.

Obviously, I'm not trying to be a people pleaser! No, I am trying to please God. If I were still trying to please people, I would not be Christ's servant.

Dear brothers and sisters, I solemnly assure you that the Good News of salvation which I preach is not based on mere human reasoning or logic. For my message came by a direct revelation from Jesus Christ himself. No one else taught me.

You know what I was like when I followed the Jewish religion—how I violently persecuted the Christians. I did my best to get rid of them. I was one of the most religious Jews of my own age, and I tried as hard as possible to follow all the old traditions of my religion.

But then something happened! For it pleased God in his kindness to choose me and call me, even before I was born! What undeserved mercy! Then he revealed his Son to me so that I could proclaim the Good News about Jesus to the Gentiles. When all this happened to me, I did not rush out to consult with anyone else; nor did I go up to Jerusalem to consult with those who were apostles before I was. No, I went away into Arabia and later returned to the city of Damascus. It was not until three years later that I finally went to Jerusalem for a visit with Peter and stayed there with him for fifteen days. And the only other apostle I met at that time was James, our Lord's brother. You must believe what I am saying, for I declare before God that I am not lying. Then after this visit, I went north into the provinces of Syria and Cilicia. And still the Christians in the churches in Judea didn't know me personally. All they knew was that people were saying, "The one who used to persecute us now preaches the very faith he tried to destroy!" And they gave glory to God because of me.

Then fourteen years later I went back to Jerusalem again, this time with Barnabas; and Titus came along, too. I went there because God revealed to me that I should go. While I was there I talked privately with the leaders of the church. I wanted them to understand what I had been preaching to the Gentiles. I wanted to make sure they did not disagree, or my ministry would have been useless. And they did agree. They did not even demand that my companion Titus be circumcised, though he was a Gentile.

Even that question wouldn't have come up except for some so-called Christians there—false ones, really—who came to spy on us and see our freedom in Christ Jesus. They wanted to force us, like slaves, to follow their Jewish regulations. But we refused to listen to them for a single moment. We wanted to preserve the truth of the Good News for you.

And the leaders of the church who were there had nothing to add to what I was preaching. (By the way, their reputation as great leaders made no difference to me, for God has no favorites.) They saw that God had given me the responsibility of preaching the Good News to the Gentiles, just as he had given Peter the responsibility of preaching to the Jews. For the same God who worked through Peter for the benefit of the Jews worked through me for the benefit of the Gentiles. In fact, James, Peter, and John, who were known as pillars of the church, recognized the gift God had given me, and they accepted Barnabas and me as their co-workers. They encouraged us to keep preaching to the Gentiles, while they continued their work with the Jews. The only thing they suggested was that we remember to help the poor, and I have certainly been eager to do that.

But when Peter came to Antioch, I had to oppose him publicly, speaking strongly against what he was doing, for it was very wrong. When he first arrived, he ate with the Gentile Christians, who don't bother with circumcision. But afterward, when some Jewish friends of James came, Peter wouldn't eat with the Gentiles anymore because he was afraid of what these legalists would say. Then the other Jewish Christians followed Peter's hypocrisy, and even Barnabas was influenced to join them in their hypocrisy.

When I saw that they were not following the truth of the Good News, I said to Peter in front of all the others, "Since you, a Jew by birth, have discarded the Jewish laws and are living like a Gentile, why are you trying to make these Gentiles obey the Jewish laws you abandoned? You and I are Jews by birth, not 'sinners' like the Gentiles. And yet we Jewish Christians know that we become right with God, not by doing what the law commands, but by faith in Jesus Christ. So we have believed in Christ Jesus, that we might be accepted by God because of our faith in Christ—and not because we have obeyed the law. For no one will ever be saved by obeying the law."

But what if we seek to be made right with God through faith in Christ and then find out that we are still sinners? Has Christ led us into sin? Of course not! Rather, I make myself guilty if I rebuild the old system I already tore down. For when I tried to keep the law, I realized I could never earn God's approval. So I died to the law so that I might live for God. I have been crucified with Christ. I myself no longer live, but Christ lives in me. So I live my life in this earthly body by trusting in the Son of God, who loved me and gave himself for me. I am not one of those who treats the grace of God as meaningless. For if we could be saved by keeping the law, then there was no need for Christ to die.

Oh, foolish Galatians! What magician has cast an evil spell on you? For you used to see the meaning of Jesus Christ's death as clearly as though I had shown you a signboard with a picture of Christ dying on the cross. Let me ask you this one question: Did you receive the Holy Spirit by keeping the law? Of course not, for the Holy Spirit came upon you only after you believed the message you heard about Christ. Have you lost your senses? After starting your Christian lives in the Spirit, why are you now trying to become perfect by your own human effort? You have suffered so much for the Good News. Surely it was not in vain, was it? Are you now going to just throw it all away?

I ask you again, does God give you the Holy Spirit and work miracles among you because you obey the law of Moses? Of course not! It is because you believe the message you heard about Christ.

In the same way, "Abraham believed God, so God declared him righteous because of his faith." The real children of Abraham, then, are all those who put their faith in God.

What's more, the Scriptures looked forward to this time when God would accept the Gentiles, too, on the basis of their faith. God promised this good news to Abraham long ago when he said, "All nations will be blessed through you." And so it is: All who put their faith in Christ share the same blessing Abraham received because of his faith.

But those who depend on the law to make them right with God are under his curse, for the Scriptures say, "Cursed is everyone who does not observe and obey all these commands that are written in God's Book of the Law." Consequently, it is clear that no one can ever be right with God by trying to keep the law. For the Scriptures say, "It is through faith that a righteous person has life." How different from this way of faith is the way of law, which says, "If you wish to find life by obeying the law, you must obey all of its commands." But Christ has rescued us from the curse pronounced by the law. When he was hung on the cross, he took upon himself the curse for our wrongdoing. For it is written in the Scriptures, "Cursed is everyone who is hung on a tree." Through the work of Christ Jesus, God has blessed the Gentiles with the same blessing he promised to Abraham, and we Christians receive the promised Holy Spirit through faith.

Dear brothers and sisters, here's an example from everyday life. Just as no one can set aside or amend an irrevocable agreement, so it is in this case. God gave the promise to Abraham and his child. And notice that it doesn't say the promise was to his children, as if it meant many descendants. But the promise was to his child—and that, of course, means Christ. This is what I am trying to say: The agreement God made with Abraham could not be canceled 430 years later when God gave the law to Moses. God would be breaking his promise. For if the inheritance could be received only by keeping the law, then it would not be the result of accepting God's promise. But God gave it to Abraham as a promise.

Well then, why was the law given? It was given to show people how guilty they are. But this system of law was to last only until the coming of the child to whom God's promise was made. And there is this further difference. God gave his laws to angels to give to Moses, who was the mediator between God and the people. Now a mediator is needed if two people enter into an agreement, but God acted on his own when he made his promise to Abraham.

Well then, is there a conflict between God's law and God's promises? Absolutely not! If the law could have given us new life, we could have been made right with God by obeying it. But the Scriptures have declared that we are all prisoners of sin, so the only way to receive God's promise is to believe in Jesus Christ.

Until faith in Christ was shown to us as the way of becoming right with God, we were guarded by the law. We were kept in protective custody, so to speak, until we could put our faith in the coming Savior.

Let me put it another way. The law was our guardian and teacher to lead us until Christ came. So now, through faith in Christ, we are made right with God. But now that faith in Christ has come, we no longer need the law as our guardian. So you are all children of God through faith in Christ Jesus. And all who have been united with Christ in baptism have been made like him. There is no longer Jew or Gentile, slave or free, male or female. For you are all Christians—you are one in Christ Jesus. And now that you belong to Christ, you are the true children of Abraham. You are his heirs, and now all the promises God gave to him belong to you.

Think of it this way. If a father dies and leaves great wealth for his young children, those children are not much better off than slaves until they grow up, even though they actually own everything their father had. They have to obey their guardians until they reach whatever age their father set.

And that's the way it was with us before Christ came. We were slaves to the spiritual powers of this world. But when the right time came, God sent his Son, born of a woman, subject to the law. God sent him to buy freedom for us who were slaves to the law, so that he could adopt us as his very own children. And because you Gentiles have become his children, God has sent the Spirit of his Son into your hearts, and now you can call God your dear Father. Now you are no longer a slave but God's own child. And since you are his child, everything he has belongs to you.

Before you Gentiles knew God, you were slaves to so-called gods that do not even exist. And now that you have found God (or should I say, now that God has found you), why do you want to go back again and become slaves once more to the weak and useless spiritual powers of this world? You are trying to find favor with God by what you do or don't do on certain days or months or seasons or years. I fear for you. I am afraid that all my hard work for you was worth nothing. Dear brothers and sisters, I plead with you to live as I do in freedom from these things, for I have become like you Gentiles were—free from the law.

You did not mistreat me when I first preached to you. Surely you remember that I was sick when I first brought you the Good News of Christ. But even though my sickness was revolting to you, you did not reject me and turn me away. No, you took me in and cared for me as though I were an angel from God or even Christ Jesus himself. Where is that joyful spirit we felt together then? In those days, I know you would gladly have taken out your own eyes and given them to me if it had been possible. Have I now become your enemy because I am telling you the truth?

Those false teachers who are so anxious to win your favor are not doing it for your good. They are trying to shut you off from me so that you will pay more attention to them. Now it's wonderful if you are eager to do good, and especially when I am not with you. But oh, my dear children! I feel as if I am going through labor pains for you again, and they will continue until Christ is fully developed in your lives. How I wish I were there with you right now, so that I could be more gentle with you. But at this distance I frankly don't know what else to do.

Listen to me, you who want to live under the law. Do you know what the law really says? The Scriptures say that Abraham had two sons, one from his slave-wife and one from his freeborn wife. The son of the slave-wife was born in a human attempt to bring about the fulfillment of God's promise. But the son of the freeborn wife was born as God's own fulfillment of his promise.

Now these two women serve as an illustration of God's two covenants. Hagar, the slave-wife, represents Mount Sinai where people first became enslaved to the law. And now Jerusalem is just like Mount Sinai in Arabia, because she and her children live in slavery. But Sarah, the free woman, represents the heavenly Jerusalem. And she is our mother. That is what Isaiah meant when he prophesied,

"Rejoice, O childless woman!
Break forth into loud and joyful song,
even though you never gave birth to a child.
For the woman who could bear no children
now has more than all the other women!"

And you, dear brothers and sisters, are children of the promise, just like Isaac. And we who are born of the Holy Spirit are persecuted by those who want us to keep the law, just as Isaac, the child of promise, was persecuted by Ishmael, the son of the slave-wife.

But what do the Scriptures say about that? "Get rid of the slave and her son, for the son of the slave woman will not share the family inheritance with the free woman's son." So, dear brothers and sisters, we are not children of the slave woman, obligated to the law. We are children of the free woman, acceptable to God because of our faith.

So Christ has really set us free. Now make sure that you stay free, and don't get tied up again in slavery to the law.

Listen! I, Paul, tell you this: If you are counting on circumcision to make you right with God, then Christ cannot help you. I'll say it again. If you are trying to find favor with God by being circumcised, you must obey all of the regulations in the whole law of Moses. For if you are trying to make yourselves right with God by keeping the law, you have been cut off from Christ! You have fallen away from God's grace.

But we who live by the Spirit eagerly wait to receive everything promised to us who are right with God through faith. For when we place our faith in Christ Jesus, it makes no difference to God whether we are circumcised or not circumcised. What is important is faith expressing itself in love.

You were getting along so well. Who has interfered with you to hold you back from following the truth? It certainly isn't God, for he is the one who called you to freedom. But it takes only one wrong person among you to infect all the others—a little yeast spreads quickly through the whole batch of dough! I am trusting the Lord to bring you back to believing as I do about these things. God will judge that person, whoever it is, who has been troubling and confusing you.

Dear brothers and sisters, if I were still preaching that you must be circumcised—as some say I do—why would the Jews persecute me? The fact that I am still being persecuted proves that I am still preaching salvation through the cross of Christ alone. I only wish that those troublemakers who want to mutilate you by circumcision would mutilate themselves.

For you have been called to live in freedom—not freedom to satisfy your sinful nature, but freedom to serve one another in love. For the whole law can be summed up in this one command: "Love your neighbor as yourself." But if instead of showing love among yourselves you are always biting and devouring one another, watch out! Beware of destroying one another.

So I advise you to live according to your new life in the Holy Spirit. Then you won't be doing what your sinful nature craves. The old sinful nature loves to do evil, which is just opposite from what the Holy Spirit wants. And the Spirit gives us desires that are opposite from what the sinful nature desires. These two forces are constantly fighting each other, and your choices are never free from this conflict. But when you are directed by the Holy Spirit, you are no longer subject to the law.

When you follow the desires of your sinful nature, your lives will produce these evil results: sexual immorality, impure thoughts, eagerness for lustful pleasure, idolatry, participation in demonic activities, hostility, quarreling, jealousy, outbursts of anger, selfish ambition, divisions, the feeling that everyone is wrong except those in your own little group, envy, drunkenness, wild parties, and other kinds of sin. Let me tell you again, as I have before, that anyone living that sort of life will not inherit the Kingdom of God.

But when the Holy Spirit controls our lives, he will produce this kind of fruit in us: love, joy, peace, patience, kindness, goodness, faithfulness, gentleness, and self-control. Here there is no conflict with the law.

Those who belong to Christ Jesus have nailed the passions

and desires of their sinful nature to his cross and crucified them there. If we are living now by the Holy Spirit, let us follow the Holy Spirit's leading in every part of our lives. Let us not become conceited, or irritate one another, or be jealous of one another.

Dear brothers and sisters, if another Christian is overcome by some sin, you who are godly should gently and humbly help that person back onto the right path. And be careful not to fall into the same temptation yourself. Share each other's troubles and problems, and in this way obey the law of Christ. If you think you are too important to help someone in need, you are only fooling yourself. You are really a nobody.

Be sure to do what you should, for then you will enjoy the personal satisfaction of having done your work well, and you won't need to compare yourself to anyone else. For we are each responsible for our own conduct.

Those who are taught the word of God should help their teachers by paying them.

Don't be misled. Remember that you can't ignore God and get away with it. You will always reap what you sow! Those who live only to satisfy their own sinful desires will harvest the consequences of decay and death. But those who live to please the Spirit will harvest everlasting life from the Spirit. So don't get tired of doing what is good. Don't get discouraged and give up, for we will reap a harvest of blessing at the appropriate time. Whenever we have the opportunity, we should do good to everyone, especially to our Christian brothers and sisters.

Notice what large letters I use as I write these closing words in my own handwriting. Those who are trying to force you to be circumcised are doing it for just one reason. They don't want to be persecuted for teaching that the cross of Christ alone can save. And even those who advocate circumcision don't really keep the whole law. They only want you to be circumcised so they can brag about it and claim you as their disciples.

As for me, God forbid that I should boast about anything except the cross of our Lord Jesus Christ. Because of that cross, my interest in this world died long ago, and the world's interest in me is also long dead. It doesn't make any difference now whether we have been circumcised or not. What counts is whether we really have been changed into new and different people. May God's mercy and peace be upon all those who live by this principle. They are the new people of God.

From now on, don't let anyone trouble me with these things. For I bear on my body the scars that show I belong to Jesus.

My dear brothers and sisters, may the grace of our Lord Jesus Christ be with you all. Amen.

—COMING SOON—

The
Titus
D I A R Y

Continuing the saga of the first-century church as seen through the eyes of Titus. Following on from *The Silas Diary* in a journey that changed the history of the world.

FREE!

If you would like to receive a free copy of *Revolution*, a book that covers the first seventeen years of the Christian story, write to the author at

Gene Edwards' Ministry
P.O. Box 285
Sargent, GA 30275
1-800-827-9825

LINCOLN CHRISTIAN COLLEGE AND SEMINARY

813
E2636S

113998

3 4711 00183 7055